"She did," I insisted. "She stood in the hall, her hands on her head, and moaned and groaned until everybody was looking at her."

Tim laughed. "Typical Dayna reaction."

"After all her work to find a band for the dance, it is a blow," Mom protested.

"She embarrasses me, acting the way she does," I said.

Suddenly Dayna stormed in the front hall. "This is an emergency! We're going to try for a Los Angeles group. Why did that dumb band have to break up six weeks before our dance?"

"That's life!" Tim said. "We only had records at our dance, and we lived through it. We even had a good time."

Real Friends

by Dorothy Hole

Cover photo by John Strange

Published by Worthington Press
7099 Huntley Road, Worthington, Ohio 43085

Printed in the United States of America

10 9 8 7 6 5 4 3 2

ISBN 0-87406-341-8

To Mary Ethel Patricia

One

"HEY, Mom," I yelled, the back door slamming behind me as I raced across the porch and into the kitchen. "The band for the dance canceled!"

"She knows, Laurie," came a voice from the breakfast nook. "I told her."

I stopped short. Tim *always* gets there first with any news. Or if not Tim, Dayna. Being youngest is no fun. Disgusting, that's what it is, always being compared to Dayna or to Tim. I want to be me, not a clone of those two.

"How did Dayna take the news, Laurie?" Mom asked, her hands busy peeling an onion for the meat loaf.

"Like a moron." Dayna embarrasses me, acting the way she does.

Mom sighed. She never likes it when I criticize Dayna.

"She did," I insisted, walking over to the

refrigerator and taking out a carton of milk. "She stood in the hall, her hands on her head, and moaned and groaned until everybody was looking at her."

Tim laughed. "Typical Dayna reaction."

"After all her hard work to find a group to play at the dance, it is a blow," Mom protested.

"I'll bet Laurie has some ideas on the subject of what the dance committee should do now," Tim teased.

"Cut it out," I told him. I've got this problem. He and Dayna claim I'm always interfering. I'm not, though. They just don't know the difference between trying to help and being bossy. I only make suggestions in case nobody else has thought of my idea. That's not the same as trying to arrange everything for everybody.

I took a glass out of the cupboard and plopped down beside Tim in the breakfast nook. "You almost lost your daughter today, Mom," I announced dramatically, hoping the shock would change the subject.

"What happened?" Mom didn't sound at all worried.

"A moving van came out of the Rodney driveway and almost ran me down."

"Tim told me a new family was moving in."

Mom hastily turned on the cold water faucet. She claims you won't cry if you peel onions under cold water. It makes no difference. She cries anyway.

I made a face at Tim. Looking at him is like looking in a mirror. He has dark brown eyes, just like mine, and he has the same light brown hair we both got from Dad. But Tim has the waves, naturally, and my hair is goalpost straight.

But that's as far as our being alike goes. He's good at everything—football, playing guitar, working at the market for Mr. Hansen. And he's still a straight *A* student, even now in eleventh grade. It's depressing. I mean, *really* depressing. I don't let myself think about it.

"The new people have a kid," Tim said, turning a page of the evening paper he was reading.

Before taking a gulp of milk I demanded, "Who says?"

"They ordered a large-size jar of peanut butter."

"Well, Sherlock Holmes, that doesn't prove anything. Mom eats peanut-butter sandwiches all the time."

Tim works for Mr. Hansen at his market a couple afternoons a week after school. He works on Saturdays sometimes, too, except

9

during football season.

"It will seem strange to have the Rodney house lived in after all these years of standing empty." Mom finished with the onions and started shaping the ground meat.

I knew what she meant. The Rodney house is located right next to us. It's surrounded by three acres of orange groves. Nobody's lived in it for ages because old Mrs. Rodney's grandchildren are fighting over which one of them is the owner. The house itself looks like a small castle—a *very* small castle. But it's pretty big for a house, with its wooden turrets at the corners. Mom calles it "bad Victorian." When I was little, the stone lions guarding the entrance of the driveway frightened me. Then when I got a little older, I used to think the huge house would be a great place to play hide-and-seek.

I gave Tim my ear-to-ear grin. "Hey, Sherlock, would you take Jeannie and me to a movie tonight? There's a mystery at the Rialto."

"Nope. The band's going to practice."

That's *always* his excuse for getting out of doing things. He and two other guys call themselves the Owls. They're not the Beatles, but then again they're not bad, not that I'd admit it to them, of course.

Dayna stormed in from the front hall. She's the pretty one. Her hair is straight too, but it has a golden shine, and her eyes are blue like Mom's. Every time she tries out for anything, she wins. And she always ends up chairperson of the committee or captain of the team. That's something I'll never understand.

"Will you go with me to the movie tonight?" I asked quickly, even though I could see she was upset. Mom thinks Jeannie and I are too young to go to the movies alone.

Dayna shook her head. "I have an emergency meeting of the dance committee."

"But you said last Fri—" I began.

"This is an emergency!" She was almost screaming. Even Mom glanced up from the meat loaf.

"Why don't you guys ask the Owls to play?" Tim suggested.

Dayna shook her head again. "I mentioned them, but Lois vetoed the idea."

Tim raised his eyebrows. "Wait till I tell Luke." Luke is one of the Owls.

"That's the reason. Lois says it's her class dance, and she wants to dance, not sit around because her boyfriend plays in the band." Dayna slid onto the bench in the nook. "We want a name band."

"Like Mossy Banks!" I suggested excitedly.

"Fourteen months at the top of the charts! If you could get them, Dayna—wow!"

"Don't be stupid!" Dayna exclaimed. "I didn't mean *that* big of a name!"

Tim burst out laughing. "Ian Macpherson is just waiting for your call. He'll cancel an L.A. Forum concert to play at the Alta Vista Junior High graduation dance!"

"We're going to try for a Los Angeles group—maybe Dangerface." Dayna's voice became a moan. "Why did Fail-Safe have to break up six weeks before our dance?"

"That's life!" were Tim's sympathetic words. "We only had records at our ninth-grade graduation dance, and we lived through it. We even had a good time."

"But we've already announced live music," Dayna wailed. "After that awful job we had convincing the faculty, we have to find somebody!"

"I'm sorry about the band canceling," I told her. "I really am. Music's my thing, you know that. I can just imagine how upset you are."

"Dayna, where are you meeting?" Mom asked.

"Here."

"You remembered that we won't be here, didn't you?"

Great! That really blasted my evening. The

fourth Friday of every month my folks attend the travel series at the high school. After the lecture and film, they always go with Mr. and Mrs. Collins for dessert at the Upside Down House. I'd been going to try to talk Mom and Dad into going to the movie with us. But that was out now.

At dinner Mom told Dad about the new people moving into the Rodney house. That stirred up my curiosity again. "I wonder who they are," I said. "If the peanut-butter kid is little, maybe I can baby-sit and earn some money."

"Wonderful!" Dayna oozed sweetness. "You're such a good planner, you can save what you earn for college."

That's just like Dayna. She knows college is a "no go" with me.

"The only reason I'm not dropping out of high school," I announced, "is that Mom and Dad want me to finish."

"Glad to hear it." Dad grinned at me.

I decided that I'd better start saving to buy a car. Not that I said anything. Dad's a great guy, even if he is a dentist, but something told me he'd object if I bought an old car. He didn't even want Dayna to have one, and she's 15.

"It'll be nice to have the Rodney place lived

in," was Dad's only comment.

As usual, I ended up doing the dishes. By the time I finished, the Owls were hooting away and the dance committee had moved up to Dayna's room because they couldn't hear each other talk downstairs.

Just as I curled up in the big overstuffed chair in the living room, all set to watch the Owls rehearse, Tim ordered, "Run along, little girl. This is a serious practice session."

"I won't make any noise. Honest, I won't."

"Out!" Tim pointed toward the entrance hall as if I were some sort of pet dog.

"This is my living room, too!" I flung over my shoulder as I marched out of the room and headed for the kitchen. *Guys!* I thought. *I hate guys!* They're either little twerps like the ones in my class or dictators like Tim.

I struggled to my room with a bag of chocolate-chip cookies, three diet colas from the kitchen, and the small TV from my parents' room. Then I turned on the set and flopped onto my bed. Tim and Dayna sure turn my life into Dullsville. I couldn't even watch TV in peace with Luke banging away on the drums. If I had a choice, I'd be an only child.

What a way to spend a Friday night—alone in a house full of people. *Nuts,* I thought, climbing off the bed and going down the hall and pushing open the door of Dayna's room.

"Get out. You're not on the committee," she greeted me.

"I got kicked out by the Owls."

"Go study. You could use some time doing that."

I just stood there, looking sad.

"Out!" Dayna insisted, sounding just like Tim.

"Oh, let her stay," Lois said.

"I won't say anything," I promised, sitting cross-legged on the floor.

There were four girls in the meeting besides Dayna.

"No guys?" I asked.

"This is an ad hoc committee. The full committee meets tomorrow. We're just making recommendations."

"Oh," I said, pretending I knew what *ad hoc* meant.

For an emergency meeting, they were getting nowhere. Their recommendations ranged from the "impossible" (Ian Macpherson and Mossy Banks) to the "maybe possible" (Dangerface) to the "definitely possible" that nobody wanted (the Owls).

This was a dumb meeting. Finally I said, "Why don't you guys just write to Mossy

Banks and find out if they can come on such short notice?" Dayna and I sure are different. If I were Dayna, I'd have the envelope sealed and stamped by now.

"Why don't we?" Lois asked. "You're chairperson, Dayna, so you could sign the letter."

"The guys will be mad if we go ahead without them," Suzy, one of the committee members, warned.

"Ha!" I laughed sarcastically. "They'll be mad if you get Ian Macpherson? Not on your life!"

"Get out!" Dayna yelled, repeating herself.

Then I left. The argument over how to word the letter—if they decided to send one—was stupid. It embarrassed me to have Dayna for a sister when she acted so dumb.

Just as I wandered into my room, the phone rang. I raced to grab it in my parents' room.

"I thought we were going to a movie," Jeannie said. Jeannie Collins has been my best friend since we were little kids.

"I'm marooned," I explained to the accompaniment of ear-wounding thunder.

"Hey, are the Owls at your house?"

"No," I answered. "That's the London Symphony in our living room."

"Very funny. At least you're not stuck babysitting eight-year-old twins." She exaggerated,

urse, since her grandmother, who lives
hem, is the one who's stuck with the
most of the time.

just as soon be with you," I told her.
been kicked out by the Owls, and the
committee meeting's a bore."

n we talked about some of the guys in
ass, mostly about Kevin. My heart does
stics whenever he's around. He's
ed his field of interest to Jeannie in the
w weeks. That hurts, but she's my best
so I can't let her know how much it
s me. I'll have to learn to live with an
heart, I guess.

a while I heard her doorbell and then
ndmother's voice calling, "Jeannie, you
have visitors."

"See you tomorrow at the tennis courts,"
Jeannie said hurriedly. "Same time as usual."
She hung up, leaving me to wonder who had
stopped by to see her.

There wasn't anything on TV I wanted to
watch, and I sure wasn't going to do Monday's
homework assignments, even if Dayna did
think I should hit the books. No matter how
much I studied, my grades would never match
hers or Tim's. I debated reading a book, but
that smacked too much of school.

I decided to watch TV anyway. I went over

to close the window shades and noticed a light in the Rodney house where there hadn't been one for years. Even though I knew that new people had moved in, just for a moment it surprised me.

"Why couldn't someone interesting move in," I asked myself, "instead of a peanut-butter kid? Someone interesting," I sighed. "Someone like Kevin!"

Two

LUCK was on my side because I hadn't changed into my pajamas yet when the doorbell rang. "Laurie, come on down," Tim called. "Bob Ridgeway is here."

I went to the top of the staircase. "Bub doesn't want"—instead of looking down at Tim, my eyes gazed right into Bob's—"to see me," I ended lamely.

Bob's face turned red. I hadn't meant to be mean. His nickname had just slipped out. Bob had always been the fat kid in our class. Way back in kindergarten, someone had claimed he was as round as a bubble, and he'd been known as Bubble or Bub ever since. He didn't like it then, and now in seventh grade, he loathed it.

I came down the stairs, wishing with each step it were Kevin at the bottom. "Hi," I said.

His bright crimson face faded into a pale

pink. "I heard you didn't go to the movie and thought you might like company."

"Sure," I said, sighing deeply. "That's why you've got your camera with you, I suppose."

Bob looked puzzled. "I always carry it. You know that."

"Right." I nodded.

The lines on his forehead deepened into a frown. "What's that supposed to mean?"

"You just happened to come over after Jeannie just happened to mention that the Owls and the dance committee are here."

He stared at me. "Is that what you think? You really believe I came over because the Owls and the committee are here?" He shook his head slowly from side to side. "Boy, have you got a problem! Next time I'll know better!" He turned and headed for the front door.

All Bob had ever wanted was to be a photographer on the school paper. He was out to prove himself because the paper's staff regarded seventh-graders as nonhumans. True, wherever Bob went, he lugged along his camera. It was just a fact of junior-high life that he spent his days looking for a scoop.

"Wait up," I said without thinking, knowing I hadn't been very nice.

"I have hundreds of pictures of the Owls and of the dance committee," Bob continued.

"I don't need any more."

"I was going to make some brownies," I lied. "Want to help?"

He thought for a moment.

"Why not?" Shrugging, he put his camera on the hall table and followed me to the kitchen.

I motioned toward the stove. "Turn on the oven, will you?"

While I gathered the brownie mix and pan and the rest of the things we needed, I asked, "How come you guys didn't go to the movie tonight?"

"Kevin called Jeannie to see what was going on. She said you hadn't let her know about a ride so she guessed you'd be staying home. We stopped in at her house, and then I thought I'd come over here. How high do you want the oven?"

"Set it at 350°," I answered. "We're hoping to go see the movie tomorrow."

"Yeah, that's what Jeannie said."

So, I thought, *Kevin is over at Jeannie's, and I'm stuck with Bob, better known as Bubble.*

Just then I heard an earsplitting drum blast.

"Luke sure is in good form tonight," Bob commented. "Have you ever been to a rock concert?"

"No, but I sure would love to go to one."

"I went to the L.A. Forum to hear Mossy

21

Banks. Ian Macpherson is the greatest."

We talked about rock music for a while.

When the oven timer buzzed, it surprised me. The time had gone so fast.

Bob took a plate of brownies in to the Owls while I carried some up to the dance committee. When I came down, Bob was sitting on the next-to-bottom step, so I sat beside him. We kept on talking about bands and nibbling on brownies.

It seemed like only a few minutes, but it must have been longer. The dance committee had started to drift toward the first floor, and the Owls had already packed up their instruments when the front door swung open.

Mom came dancing in, swaying back and forth. "Kids, I have some news for you," she announced. "I'm running away to the Greek Isles immediately after breakfast tomorrow."

"Please notice, she's going on a full stomach," Dad teased.

"She's like this every month after the travel film," I explained to Bob. "In the last year, she's threatened to desert us for France, Hawaii, Brazil, and Japan."

"Come on, Bob," Tim interrupted. "I'll drive you home. It's too late for you to ride your bike."

"Maybe I'll see you tomorrow," Bob said as

he went out the door with the mob, leaving me in an empty house.

After I showered, I crawled under the blankets and gazed wide-eyed at the ceiling. Of course, it had been the wrong guy, but the evening hadn't been bad at all. *But,* I thought, *sharing brownies with Kevin instead of Bob would have made it perfect.*

My plan to stay in bed the next morning until ten-thirty was squashed by Jeannie's phone call.

"You can't sleep over tonight," she said.

I yawned. "Why not?"

"Some dumb cousin from Chicago called. He's in California and wants to drop in on his way to San Francisco. Mom talked him into staying overnight," Jeannie said. "How did it go with Bob?"

"Okay. How about you and Kevin?" It hurt to ask.

"Awful!" she wailed. "Absolutely awful! The twins bugged us every minute. It was like a horror film!"

"Gee, that's a shame," I sympathized.

A couple of hours later, as I bicycled to the tennis courts, Tim drove by in Mr. Hansen's van on his way to make a grocery delivery. He honked at me as he turned into the Rodney driveway.

When I got to the courts, I saw Jeannie acting goofy with the guys. We're best friends and all that, but Jeannie sure has changed in seventh grade. Whenever guys come along, she gets all giggly. It gives me the creeps to watch her.

"Hi, Laurie," she said, giggling. "Kevin and Bob want to play doubles with us."

Bob swung his camera strap off his shoulder. "If it's okay with you, Laurie."

"Sure." I knew, of course, whose partner I'd be. As Kevin looked at Jeannie and smiled, I wondered what would happen if I became a giggler, too.

"Hey, Laurie," Kevin called across the net before Jeannie served. "What band are they getting for the graduation dance?"

"I don't know," I answered.

"Well, who are they *trying* to get?"

"I don't know. I'm not on the committee."

"But your sister's the chairman."

"Chairperson," I growled.

He's like that. Once Kevin starts on a subject, he can drive you crazy with his questions. That's his only flaw. Even Mr. Rodriguez, the science teacher, who claims that an inquisitive mind is the basis of all knowledge, wishes Kevin would shut up most of the time.

The tennis game was yucky. Jeannie wasn't

24

at her best. Maybe it was because of Kevin. After a while, she asked the guys to go back to her house for hot dogs.

Jeannie lives in a ranch-style house, all on one floor. We went back to her room, and Kevin put on an Ian Macpherson tape. Jeannie has the best record and tape collection of any of us. Her dad owns the music store.

With the volume turned up, we invaded the kitchen and fixed ourselves lunch. Then we settled down on the patio to listen to the tape while we ate.

"Come on, Laurie, tell us who's playing at the dance." Kevin's questions are like a virus with no known cure.

I wanted Kevin to talk to me, but not because of a dopey dance Dayna was in charge of. Finally I said, "Wait and see!" I lowered my voice and added, "You'll be surprised."

At that moment, Bob went inside to put on another Ian Macpherson tape. When he got back he asked, "When's the new Mossy Banks album being released?"

"Middle of May." Jeannie supplied the information. "Dad says it will make great graduation presents. It's called 'The Nile.'"

"Let's get Ian and Mossy Banks for our graduation dance two years from now," Bob suggested happily.

"It would take a million bucks," Kevin said.

I wondered if Dayna and her committee had written to Mossy Banks. Her class treasury had $225 to spend. Maybe Ian Macpherson could consider the ninth-grade dance a charity gig.

That thought kept nagging me the rest of the afternoon. Around three o'clock the eight-year-old twins came barging in like a hurricane, their arms full of books from the library. The guys left shortly after that, and before long Tim showed up in the station wagon. He lifted my bike into the back, and I put my tennis racket on the floor.

We were riding along, my thoughts still on Ian Macpherson, when Tim said, "I made a date for you for tomorrow. I told Mrs. Logan you'd play tennis with her granddaughter."

"You what?" I demanded. There is nothing that turns me into a hostile nonhuman faster than when Tim and Dayna tell people I'll do something before they ask me. You can imagine what would happen if *I* tried that trick on *them!*

"And who is Mrs. Logan?" I continued.

"She's the one who rented the Rodney place. Her granddaughter Stacey is your age."

"Well, I don't care who she is," I said, trying out my snarl. I couldn't let Tim know it sounded interesting, so I glared at him—a wasted glare because he was watching the road. "Why couldn't you have asked me before you promised I'd do it? Why should I play tennis with a complete stranger? I have plenty of friends I can ask if I feel like playing tomorrow. And when am I supposed to get my homework done?"

"Simmer down." He laughed. "It's no big deal. Stacey doesn't know anyone here, so I thought it would be nice for her to see one familiar face on Monday when she starts at the junior high. Knowing how you like to manage things, I'll bet you'll arrange it so she'll know the whole school by nightfall." He gave me a quick glance. "And since when do you worry about homework?"

We rode in silence the rest of the way.

As we pulled into the driveway, Tim said, "Stacey seems very shy."

"Oh, great!" After Tim turned off the motor, I got out and slammed the door shut to show him how disgusted I was.

In the kitchen, Mom said to me, "You're the only one home for supper, so I thought we'd have your favorite—spaghetti."

"Thanks, Mom," I told her. I couldn't stop worrying about what Stacey would be like.

Dayna popped in briefly to change into a

clean pair of jeans and trade her T-shirt for a blouse.

"What happened at the meeting?" I flopped on her bed.

"We've asked some of the groups in Los Angeles," she said.

"What about Mossy Banks? I thought you were going to try to get them."

"Don't be ridiculous! Superstars wouldn't be interested in our little dance!"

The royal put-down. I should have had more sense than to carry on a conversation with her. I stomped out of her room.

In my own room, I did a flying leap onto my bed and then propped up my chin in my hands. She was right, of course. A superstar like Ian Macpherson just doesn't perform at junior-high-school dances. But I couldn't understand why the committee hadn't at least written to him. It would be fun to get a letter from him. So what if Mossy Banks couldn't make it. Why not at least ask?

I rolled over onto my back and studied the ceiling. Bob's suggestion kept bouncing around my brain. Why not get Mossy Banks for our junior-high graduation dance? It really was a fantastic idea. And it gave me two years to work out details—the million bucks, for instance.

Three

WATCHING a dumb rerun on TV and trying to figure out how to get a million dollars in two years are not my favorite things to do on a Saturday night. So when the phone rang, I ran to get it. I thought it might be Jeannie.

"Is this the Hamilton residence?" a strange voice asked, surprising me.

"Yes," I answered, hoping it wasn't an emergency for Dad.

"This is Mrs. Logan, Stacey's grandmother. You must be Laurie."

At first I drew a blank. Then I remembered—the Rodney place. I nodded and then realized she couldn't see over the phone.

"Yes, I'm Laurie," I said.

"I called to speak with your mother. Is she busy?"

"Well, she's watching TV and at the commercials she's doing needlepoint."

Mrs. Logan laughed. "Well, don't bother her then. I just wanted to confirm your date with Stacey tomorrow. I hope you're free to come."

"Oh, sure. Tim told me about it. He said two o'clock."

"That's fine. Do you know where we live?"

"Right next door," I told her.

"That's convenient. Stacey and I think we're going to enjoy living here. Have you always lived next to the Rodneys?"

"Ever since I was born." I started to say good-bye, but she continued.

"And your parents—have they always lived here, too?"

"Mom has, but Dad grew up in Chicago. He moved to California when he was 12."

The lady laughed again. "You might say he's almost a native." She paused, making me wonder what the next question would be. "So then your parents have known each other since they were children?"

"Oh, no," I said. "They met in college. Dad roomed with Uncle Joe."

I felt like a suspect on a *Hill Street Blues* rerun. I mean, if she wanted to ask about me, or even about school, I could understand. But her questions were weird.

"Uncle Joe is my mom's brother," I volunteered.

"I see. Does your father work close by?"

Her questions began to bug me. "He's a dentist," I answered. And being loyal to Dad, I added, "He's a good one, too."

"I'm sure he is. Please tell your mother I called," she said, ending the quiz. "I've enjoyed talking with you, Laurie. Stacey is looking forward to your game tomorrow. Good-bye."

I walked back to the family room, trying to figure out what that was all about. Mom glanced up from her needlepoint.

"Is something wrong?"

I shook my head. "That was Mrs. Logan. She just wanted to check to see if I really am coming over to meet Stacey. But she sure asked a lot of questions."

"You can't blame her," Mom said. "After all, she's new here and doesn't know us. She probably wanted to find out something about you before you showed up."

"But that's just it," I said. "All she wanted to know was about you and Dad. She didn't seem at all interested in me."

Dad peered over the top of his glasses. "Did she give us an *A* for approved?"

"She didn't cancel our date. If she wants to,

it's okay with me. I'll meet her granddaughter at school on Monday, anyway."

All those questions made me uneasy. By bedtime I almost called Mrs. Logan to say I couldn't make it after all. But I couldn't think of a good excuse.

* * * * *

At two o'clock the next afternoon I pedaled my bike between the watch-lions guarding the driveway. Tim still annoyed me, but not as much as I pretended. He had made it possible for me to get into the Rodney house, and I might never get invited again. I planned to take a good look around.

Years ago, when I was small, I thought the Rodney house was haunted because it was always dark and no one lived there. Now that I'm older, it still seems different from other houses.

As I got closer, I could see how run-down the house was. "Who'd want to live here?" I asked myself as I rounded a curve.

A man wearing a plaid jacket, a yellow sports shirt, and brown trousers pushed himself out of a lounge chair. He stepped right in front of me, blocking my way. He looked to be almost ten feet tall, though probably he only measured about six.

"Hi, I'm John."

"Hi," I answered. We just looked at each other. *He must be around 30,* I decided. He had wrinkles at the corners of his brown eyes and looked like he spent a lot of time outdoors.

"What's your name?" he asked.

"Laurie. Laurie Hamilton."

"Oh, yes. I met your brother yesterday. I'm glad you came to meet Stacey." He started walking with me toward the house.

The front door opened as we went up the steps to the house. A woman with lots of gray in her hair smiled at me.

"You must be Laurie. It's nice of you to come," she said as she pulled the door back so I could walk past her. "I'm Mrs. Logan."

The entrance hall was dark after the outside glare, and it took a couple of seconds before I could really see. Brown paneling went about halfway up the walls, and wallpaper with a faded design covered the top section up to the ceiling. Through an archway on the left I saw a living room. Through another arch to the right was the dining room. At the end of the hall was a curving staircase. A girl started coming down the stairs.

She had on a white tennis dress, and her

skinny legs ended in tennis socks with puffs at the heels and tennis shoes. None of the kids I knew dressed like that. I felt like a nerd in my cut-off jeans.

As she walked toward me, I got this strange feeling that I had met her before. But how could I know her?

"Laurie, this is my granddaughter, Stacey."

"Hi." I put as much pep into my voice as I could. I'd have much rather been with Jeannie. Tim sure had messed up my Sunday afternoon.

"Hello." Stacey spoke in a low voice.

All of them were studying me, making me feel like a stuffed animal in a museum.

"Well," I said, "do you have a bike, or do you want to walk to the high school?"

"Oh, Granny, may I?" Stacey looked like I always feel when I know that Mom is going to say no.

Mrs. Logan's lips parted in a smile. "Another time, perhaps. Poor Mr. Green and his Evergreen Gardeners worked so hard to clear the weeds from the tennis court. They'll be disappointed if you don't play there today."

"Don't forget how I struggled to put up the net," John added.

Stacey started toward the door, her shoulders drooping.

"Have a good game," Mrs. Logan called as I followed Stacey down the steps.

We walked silently. Stacey didn't look quite as plain as she had inside. Her light brown hair was shiny and bouncy. It glowed with red highlights in the sunshine.

"It must be fun to have your own tennis court." I just made conversation to break the silence. "Are you a good player?"

She shrugged. "So-so." A few steps later she asked, "Are you?"

"Nope," I answered truthfully. "My sister, Dayna, is captain of the tennis team. She and my brother are great, but I'm like you, so-so."

The tennis court had so many holes in it where the weeds that had grown through the asphalt surface had been yanked out. It looked as though it was just getting over the chicken pox. And the net—well, tennis nets are supposed to be full of holes, but not the kind this one had! Its holes would easily let through a basketball.

"I'm sorry," Stacey murmured, her face turning an embarrassed red. I didn't blame her. The court was a mess.

"How long since anyone used it?" I asked.

"Granny doesn't know. She's going to have it resurfaced this week, and John is buying a new net. He found this one in the garage."

After we batted the ball around a few times, I knew that her *so-so* and my *terrific* meant the same thing. She had the same intense look on her face that Dayna gets when she plays. I hadn't wanted to come, and now I found myself up against a future pro. I promised myself that when Tim and Dayna left home and I could lead my own life, I'd never make tennis dates with strangers.

The beginning of the game went okay, even though Stacey outmatched me each play. Then the ball bounced through one of the holes and accidentally hit my racket. I burst out laughing. The ball had shot back at Stacey so quickly that I don't think she'd realized what happened.

From then on, I started aiming at the holes just for fun. Some I hit, more I missed. When Stacey caught on to what I was doing, she narrowed her eyes and gave me a look like Mr. Franklin gives me when I make up an answer to one of his history questions.

Stacey's ball started hitting the holes too, "accidentally on purpose." At first I figured she'd made a mistake, but then I realized she couldn't be aiming wrong that many times. Talk about crazy games—this one was wild.

We both started giggling. Soon my side hurt from laughing. I collapsed onto the ground while Stacey staggered to the net and leaned over. She had trouble breathing, she was laughing so hard.

Finally she said, "Let's go up to the house. I'm thirsty."

I scrambled to my feet and trotted beside her. We passed John in his lounge chair under a tree. He put down the book he was reading and waved as we went by.

"Who is John?"

We took a few steps before Stacey answered. "He's just a friend who's staying with us a little while to help Granny get settled."

"Oh," I said. Then I asked, "How come you're moving here now, in the middle of a school term, instead of waiting until the new term starts?"

Stacey got a really funny look on her face that I couldn't figure out. "My grandmother's some kind of cousin to the Rodneys, and she wanted to."

"Have you always lived with your grandmother?" I was beginning to sound like Kevin with all my questions.

Stacey shook her head. "No. Only recently." Before I could ask another question, she got one in. "Do you take your lunch or eat in the school cafeteria?"

"I brown-bag it," I told her while she walked ahead and opened the back door.

Peeking under a covered plate in the kitchen, Stacey announced, "Cookies. You take these, and I'll bring some juice."

She grabbed the juice and some glasses and led the way to the entrance hall. We almost bumped into a roly-poly woman coming through the doorway.

"Laurie, I'd like you to meet Aunt Martha." Stacey nodded toward the woman.

"Hi," I greeted her.

Aunt Martha noticed the plate in my hand. "Here, let me take those for you."

She reached out her hands, but I thanked her and said, "We can manage okay."

After the door swung shut, I frowned, thinking that Stacey and the woman didn't look at all alike. "She's your aunt?"

"She's not a blood relative. 'Aunt' is a courtesy title, Granny calls it."

Weird, I thought. *Stacey lives with her grandmother, a no-relation aunt, and a friend named John, but no parents. Some families sure do get mixed up,* I thought, remembering some of the kids at school whose parents are divorced.

We sat on a screened porch on the side of the house. As we drank apple juice and ate chocolate-chip cookies, I fielded her questions about school.

I explained that Alta Vista Junior High is made up of seventh, eighth, and ninth grades. I told her that my sister, Dayna, was in ninth grade. "Dayna's head of the committee for the graduation dance. The dance is for the whole school but only ninth graders plan it." Then I told her about the band canceling at the last moment.

"And, of course, there's the *News*. It comes out twice a month. It's pretty much run by the ninth graders, too, but one of the guys in my homeroom, Bob Ridgeway, is a camera freak and gets some of his pictures in it now and then." I almost told her about Kevin, but I bit my tongue. I had only just met Stacey, and the way I felt about Kevin was still a secret.

"What's Bob like?" she asked shyly.

"Oh, I guess he's okay," I answered, stuffing a cookie into my mouth.

She wanted to know about Tim. I told her that he was a junior in high school. When I mentioned the Owls, Stacey wrinkled up her nose as though she had smelled something bad.

"I've never been in the Rodney house before," I went on, wiping the crumbs from my mouth with a paper napkin.

39

"Want to see my room?"

"Sure," I said, following Stacey up the stairs.

What a room! It was yellow with white furniture. There was a four-poster bed with a canopy over it, a dressing table with a flounce, a desk, a chaise, a night table, and a huge stereo system. Naturally, I headed for the stereo. Stacey had albums and cassettes and CDs. It was a bigger collection than Jeannie's.

"Who's your favorite?" I asked.

"Mozart."

"Mozart!" That really made my jaw drop!

"Who's yours?" she came back at me.

I almost said Beethoven. I wouldn't know a Beethoven symphony if I heard one, but after Mozart rock 'n' roll seemed so klutzy.

Sure as anything, I'd trip myself up if I lied, so I took a deep breath and confessed, "Ian Macpherson and Mossy Banks. I'm really into rock music."

"I like rock, too."

"You do!" I exclaimed. "Somehow Mozart and rock don't seem to go together."

"Why not?" she challenged. "I like to play tennis, and I like to swim. They're both sports, but they're not at all alike. So why shouldn't I like different kinds of music?"

"I guess I just never thought about it that

way," I said meekly.

"As a matter of fact"—she paused and then confided in a soft voice—"Ian Macpherson is my favorite, too."

Just then I noticed the clock on the night table.

"Yipes! It's almost five, and I haven't done my homework. I have to go." Not that I really studied very hard, but I wanted to make a good impression.

Stacey walked downstairs and to the front door with me. I thought about all the snide remarks Dayna had made about me trying to boss everyone. Dayna was just the type to say something nasty if I showed up at school in the morning with Stacey in tow. But Tim wanted me to be nice, and I'd had a fun afternoon, so I asked Stacey, "Want to go with me to school in the morning?"

"I'll find out from Granny." Stacey raced up the stairs.

I looked around some more while Stacey was gone. I thought she'd make an all right friend. From the way her shoulders drooped as she walked back to me, I knew Mrs. Logan had said no.

"I have to register and all that sort of stuff," she explained. "Some other day."

"Okay. Enjoy your last day of freedom," I

called as I climbed on my bike.

To go home, all I had to do was coast down Stacey's drive, pedal along the road a little, and then go up our driveway. But I had time to think about my afternoon. That uneasy feeling I'd had during Mrs. Logan's telephone call last night came back to me, and I couldn't help but wonder why she'd been so curious about Mom and Dad.

I parked my bike in the garage and came in through the kitchen door. Dad's snores filled the air. He was asleep on the living room sofa—his favorite Sunday afternoon sport. Mom was curled up in the big chair reading a detective story. She grinned at me as I came in.

"Have a good time?" she asked.

"Yes," I told her, dropping into a chair. "Stacey lives with her grandmother, her aunt Martha, who isn't really her aunt, and a man named John, who's just a friend. Her grandmother wouldn't let her go to the tennis courts at school, so we had to play at her house."

"That was nice," Mom said. "After Stacey's been here a few days, I'm sure she'll be permitted to scoot around on her own the way you do."

I nodded my head slowly. I just wasn't

convinced. I thought of a billion questions I wanted to ask Stacey. Something seemed odd. I couldn't pinpoint what.

Mom got a quizzical look on her face. "You seem thoughtful."

"You know, Mom, I can't tell you why, but I just feel there's something weird about Stacey's family." I waited a bit and then added, "Very weird. Like in peculiar."

Four

STACEY showed up the next morning during third period, Mr. Franklin's World History class. Everyone half dozed to the drone of his voice. Everyone except Kevin, of course, who kept throwing out questions about the Russian Revolution.

Stacey's entrance sure woke up the guys in a hurry. Even Kevin lost track of his questions. Mr. Franklin told her to sit in an empty seat near the back of the room.

From then on to the end of the period, the guys squirmed in their seats so they could get a look at Stacey.

A few minutes before the bell rang, Mr. Franklin said, "Stacey, I'd like to speak to you after class." His eyes searched the room. "Will someone who is not starving offer to wait for Stacey and then escort her to the lunchroom?"

All the guys shot their arms into the air, and

some of the girls did, too.

"Mr. Franklin," I said, "Stacey's a friend of mine. I'd like to do it."

"Very well, Laurie." He cleared his throat, a sure sign of a big homework assignment. "On Friday, each of you will turn in a 300-word essay on the causes of the Russian Revolution." A groan of agony from all of us followed his words. "Any questions?" Just then the bell rang, and we started gathering up our books and stuff.

Jeannie waited with me in the hall. Pretty soon Stacey joined us with her news. "Mr. Franklin suggested you help me with the history assignment, Laurie, until I catch up with the rest of you."

"Okay," I agreed, wondering why. I'm not that great in history—or in any subject, for that matter.

Stacey had brown-bagged it like the rest of us. When we got to the lunchroom, I showed her the milk and juice machines. Jeannie hurried outside to claim the seat beside Kevin.

He and Bob had reserved places for us at our favorite table on the patio. I should have known better than to let Kevin loose with a stranger. As soon as we hauled out our lunches and compared sandwiches, Kevin started in.

He kicked off his questions with, "What

46

took you so long to register?"

"Well," Stacey began very slowly, "I live with my grandmother, so there was a mix-up because she's not my legal guardian."

"Who is?"

Bob spoke up. "Cut it out, Kevin. It's none of your business."

"That's okay," Stacey assured us. "There's no mystery. My parents are."

"Why don't you live with them?"

"My dad travels a lot, and my mom works, so they sent me to boarding school," Stacey continued. "I hated it, so I told my grandmother, and she arranged for me to live with her."

As much as I think Kevin is the greatest, I got squirmy, realizing he wouldn't stop the questions until all of us were embarrassed. He really is a nice guy. He just doesn't know when to quit.

He had no intention of quitting this time. "What does your dad do?"

Stacey nibbled on a peanut-butter-and-jelly sandwich. She waited so long to answer, I got the feeling she'd told all she wanted us to know.

Jeannie's usual smile had turned into a fake grin, since Kevin was paying so much attention to Stacey. So I thought I'd do both my friends a favor and interrupt.

"Stacey," I said, "Kevin's practicing to be a detective. So why don't you play murder victim and not answer any more questions?"

Kevin threw me a dirty look. But I'm resigned to the fact that while Jeannie is around, there's no Kevin in my future, anyway.

Just then Dayna and her lunch bunch took possession of the table in front of ours. Dayna's switch was turned on high. She waved her arms and laughed and talked nonstop. *No wonder she's thin,* I thought.

A perfect way to ruin my lunch is watching Dayna behaving like a weirdo. Thinking that Jeannie would understand, I asked her to change places with me.

"We're almost finished," she said.

I didn't really blame her of course. If I were sitting next to Kevin, I wouldn't want to move either.

"That's my sister, Dayna. She's the one who—"

"I know which one," Stacey interrupted me. "She looks like you, and she acts like you."

"Acts like me!" I screamed.

"Well, kind of like you did yesterday on the tennis court. And you really do look alike, too, except you're prettier."

"Hey, guys, a couple of hours with us is too

much for Stacey," I joked, my face turning red. No one had ever said that before. I loved the compliment. But as hard as I tried to pretend I didn't care, Stacey's words about how I acted upset me. *Me, act like Dayna?* The thought kept whirling in my brain.

* * * * *

The rest of the school day was routine boredom.

On our way to English, Stacey invited me to her house after school. "To tell me about the teachers," she said. "You know, their likes and dislikes and how to handle them." She had asked the wrong person. If I knew that, I'd be an honor student, but I told her I'd stop by.

"I have my bike. I'll pedal slowly so you can keep up with me," I added, assuming she would be walking.

"John's picking me up."

"Oh." I wondered how long that would go on.

After the last bell, during the traffic jam in the corridor by the lockers, Bob came along with his camera in his hand.

"How about a picture, Stacey? To record your first day for posterity and the *Alta Vista Junior High News*."

49

Stacey cocked her head to one side and gave Bob a crooked smile. "Not today. Some other time, maybe."

"You'll never make press photographer if you ask before you snap," Kevin said to Bob.

"But he'll make lots of friends," Stacey retorted.

Later on, when I started up the driveway, the guard-lions at Stacey's house nodded lazily at me. It was a trick of the sun and shadows, of course, but suddenly I felt happier.

Stacey was sitting on the porch steps. She stood up when she saw me coming. "Aunt Martha baked brownies for us," she greeted me as we went into the house together.

Stacey's grandmother was just coming down the stairs.

"Hi, Mrs. Logan," I said politely.

"Good afternoon, Laurie. Stacey says she enjoyed today and thinks she's going to like Alta Vista."

"I hope so. We have a pretty good bunch of kids."

Stacey got the brownies, and we headed up to her room. I draped myself on the chaise.

"Let's play some music," I suggested, leaning forward to take a brownie from the plate.

"What do you want to hear?" Stacey

squatted by the album rack.

"Ian Macpherson and Mossy Banks, of course," I answered, almost spilling the apple juice down my front.

"Which album?"

"Surprise me."

I planned to demonstrate my great knowledge. From the first four notes, I can identify every Mossy Banks song that's been recorded.

So, when I heard the opening notes, I started to say, "Touch the Night." Then I heard the next few notes, and they sounded like "Unforgettable Girl." When I didn't recognize the song, I decided Stacey had switched to another group.

"What group is that?" I demanded.

Placing her left foot behind her and bending low at the waist, Stacey giggled. "You asked for Mossy Banks. We aim to please."

I sat upright. "That's Ian Macpherson?" As soon as I heard his voice, I knew. I struggled to my feet and went over to the desk to look at the album jacket.

"THE NILE!" The brand-new album!

"But it's only April. This isn't supposed to be released until the middle of May." I quoted Jeannie quoting her dad. " 'In time for graduation presents.' "

Stacey gave me a really funny look. "Isn't it out yet?"

I crumpled onto the chaise again, the jacket in my hand. *Wait until I tell Jeannie!* I thought. *And Tim and Dayna, too! I'm going to be the first to hear the new Mossy Banks album!*

I started reading the back cover, beating time with my foot and nodding my head to the terrific rhythm. I flipped over the jacket.

There on the front a large, red, round sticker covered part of the design. Bold letters said PROMOTIONAL MATERIAL. NOT FOR SALE.

My mind whirled like a turntable. Where had Stacey gotten it?

Five

WE listened to the first song and then I couldn't hold back any longer. Waving the album jacket, I asked, "How did you get this?"

Casually, Stacey answered, "Oh, a friend of Granny's works for the record company and sometimes sends me new releases. I didn't know 'The Nile' wasn't in the stores yet."

Wow! The only gift I had ever gotten from a friend of my grandmother's was a lollipop. "Do you suppose her friend knows Ian Macpherson in person?"

Stacey shrugged. "Maybe."

That blew my mind to Mars and back, thinking about Stacey knowing someone who knows Ian Macpherson. I shoved that awe-inspiring knowledge into a corner of my brain where I could treasure it—far away from such disturbing influences as history and science.

When both sides of the record were finished, Stacey wanted a rundown on our teachers. After the new album, talking about teachers was a big letdown.

"Well," I began, "you can be sure of a big history assignment when Mr. Franklin clears his throat. If you like archery, you'll get an *A* in gym class, because Miss Lewis adores archery. On days when there's a baseball game, don't waste your time doing science homework. Mr. Rodriguez locks up his test tubes early, forgets to collect the papers, and races to the diamond. He's really batty over baseball!"

Stacey laughed. "And you told me you were the wrong person to ask about the teachers!"

"I guess I know about them, but it doesn't do me any good," I griped. "They all look at me and see Tim or Dayna. Just because I'm not as good a student as those two, they never give me decent grades." I stared right into Stacey's blue eyes. "Can you imagine what it's like, always having Mr. Rodriguez repeat like a dopey cuckoo bird, 'Tim was an *A* science student. I don't know why you don't do better.'"

Seeing that I had her full attention, I continued to grumble. "Here's another one for you. When I tried out for glee club, Mr. Wiley said, 'Dayna, of course, was a soloist, but I'm afraid you'll have to be in the chorus.' You know what I did? I just walked out and never went back."

A shudder went through my body. "I hope next year there's a whole new set of teachers who have never heard of Tim or Dayna!"

From the look on Stacey's face, somehow I just knew she understood. Then she said, "Here, have a brownie." I took the last one.

While I munched on the brownie, Stacey suggested, "Let's review tomorrow's homework."

Yuck, I thought, but she methodically started on the top book in the stack she had brought home from school. I couldn't concentrate. I wanted to get home and phone Jeannie about hearing "The Nile." And who does homework before dinner, anyway?

By the time I left, I had finished more assignments before five o'clock than I ever had in my whole life. In my hurry to reach a phone, I zoomed down the driveway like an Indy 500 racer.

At the road, I braked abruptly. A sudden pop inside my head had knocked my mind topsy-turvy. Without warning, my brain signaled, *Don't tell Jeannie.*

Why not? I wondered, and then something—who knows what—told me why.

Jeannie might tell Kevin, and that would be too much for him to handle. Pronto, nothing but questions. Poor Stacey! Kevin was already on her case, and the fact that she had a copy of "The Nile" album before the scheduled release date would really toss him into the end zone. Anyway, if anyone told Kevin, I wanted it to be me!

* * * * *

Tuesday and Wednesday limped by, not-so-instant replays of the usual, the only difference being Stacey's addition to our class. The guys flocked around her as if she were Miss America. Jeannie's nose was out of whack because Kevin kept following Stacey around.

Finally, I had one of my more brilliant inspirations. With Mom's permission, I invited both Stacey and Jeannie to dinner on Thursday. I'd told them we'd work on our history report that was due on Friday.

Mrs. Logan agreed that Stacey could come, which was a miracle, I thought. John was still picking her up after school every day. Everywhere she went, he went, too. It was weird.

When I asked Jeannie over for dinner, I got

a lot of giggles. "Kevin and I are going to the library to research the Russian Revolution," she said finally.

"For dinner?" I asked disgustedly.

"Don't be ridiculous."

And here I had been worrying that Kevin had deserted her. I pretended to be sorry that she couldn't make it. What I was sorry about was that I wasn't the one Kevin had asked.

After school on Thursday, I pedaled home, same as always, but John had to drive Stacey. When I opened the door to let her in, I noticed that John had waited to see her safely inside before he drove off. *What is it with Stacey anyway?* I wondered. *Don't they trust her out alone?* It made me kind of nervous, thinking there might be something wrong with her.

Stacey had been trained to do work before play. Working with her was like a bad dream.

"No records until we're finished," she said. No Ian Macpherson, no Rolling Stones, no Who. I had never before realized it was possible to study without my stereo going.

I was even glad when Mom walked into my room. "How about you girls taking a break"— my heart lit up like a Christmas tree—"and peeling the vegetables for dinner?" The Christmas lights blew a fuse!

Stacey's reaction was bizarre. She was so

eager to help that she zipped out my bedroom door and was halfway down the stairs before I caught up.

Mom had left a pile of potatoes on the kitchen drainboard for us. Stacey hesitated before picking one up.

"Peel away!" I said, sending a couple of pieces of potato skin into the sink. "We're almost through with that history paper, aren't we?" I asked hopefully. History is one subject I almost like, but it felt strange getting our assignment nearly done before supper.

My peeled potato sat on the drainboard while I tackled another one. Stacey was still working on her first.

The back door swung open, and Tim breezed in.

"Ah, the scullery maids," he greeted us. "Which of you lost a glass slipper at the ball last night?"

I rolled my eyes toward the ceiling and moaned, but Stacey's neck and face blazed crimson. The telephone saved us from more of Tim's humor.

"I'll get it," he announced.

I could see he'd flustered Stacey.

"Don't pay any attention to him," I said. "Seventeen-year-old guys are really strange."

The phone was under the stairs in the

entrance hall. Tim's voice called, "Laurie, grab the horn!"

I left a half-peeled potato on the drainboard. "I'll be right back, Stacey. You don't have to keep peeling if you don't want to."

"It's fun."

Fun? I wrinkled my nose.

I heard giggles coming over the receiver so I knew it had to be Jeannie. "Oh, Laurie, it was wonderful!"

"What was?" I asked, playing dumb.

"The library."

"The library? What's wonderful about shelves full of old books?"

"You know what I mean," she insisted. "Studying with Kevin."

"Oh, that!"

Jeannie thinks the correct way to speak English is to say "Kevin" every other word. I had to listen to how he puts Superman in the shade, as if I hadn't figured that one out for myself.

We left Kevin for a second. "You should be nicer to Bob," she scolded me. "Kevin"—he was back with us again—"says Bob wanted to ask you to go to the library today. But he thought you'd say no, so he didn't."

"Smart guy," I replied. Last Friday night, when Bob had come over, I'd had a good time talking about bands. But at school he's such a nerd, always lugging that camera around.

"You're still going to sleep over tomorrow night, aren't you?" Jeannie asked.

"Sure."

"We'll go to the movie. My parents have promised to take us. I think maybe the guys will be there."

"Ugh!" *What a trip,* I thought, *having to watch Kevin and Jeannie.*

I told Jeannie I had to hang up. As I pushed back the swinging door into the kitchen, I said, "That was Jeannie."

Stacey pointed toward a small heap of something on the drainboard. "All done," she said.

"What . . . ?" I froze, unable to believe my eyes. It looked like a pile of white marbles. *Potatoes?* I wondered. As I slowly walked toward the drainboard, I wondered what Mom would say. How had she peeled that much off a potato without chopping off a finger, too?

I gulped. "Gee, thanks for helping," I stammered. "Uh . . . uh . . . wait here a minute. I have a message for Mom from Jeannie's mom."

When Mom heard we were having boiled marbles for supper, one eyebrow shot up. Then she burst out laughing. "It would appear your friend Stacey has never done KP before."

That made me curious. Who ever heard of a 13-year-old who's never peeled potatoes?

* * * * *

Mom winked at me as she served dinner. The menu had changed, and a neat pile of mashed potatoes sat on each plate instead of boiled marbles.

Dayna wasn't home yet, but Mom decided to go ahead and eat without her.

It was a fun dinner. Both my parents paid a lot of attention to Stacey, and her shyness with them melted before she was even halfway through her mashed potatoes.

"How do you like living in the Rodney house?" Dad asked.

"Well," Stacey began, "it's not like any place I've ever lived before."

"It's not like any place *anyone* ever lived before," Tim said. "When I was a kid, I thought all the local witches made it their headquarters."

"If you hear any wild sounds, you may think the Halloween specialists have moved back in," Mom said. "But don't be alarmed, it will only be the Owls practicing. I hope your grandmother won't be disturbed by the noise."

"Noise?" Tim exploded. "That wonderful music?"

Everything was going along great when suddenly the front door flew open. Dayna, with her face looking like a red balloon ready to burst, raced into the dining room.

"You horrible brat!" she screamed, looking right at me so there was no mistaking who she meant. "You've ruined everything!"

"Dayna!" Dad's sharp voice sliced the air. "That's enough, young lady."

"It is not!" she yelled. "You know what that ... that ... that despicable creature has done? She's made a fool of me!"

"What did I do?" I couldn't imagine what her problem was.

"You've destroyed my life, that's all. I hate you!"

What *was* she talking about? It didn't make sense.

Six

WHEN Dayna paused for air, I shrugged my shoulders and glanced at Stacey. Her eyes were fixed on Dayna and matched the dinner plates for size.

"What did I do?"

"Do!" Dayna bellowed. "You spread the rumor that I had signed a 'surprise' band for the dance, that's what! It's all over school. Everyone's guessing that it's someone big, like Mossy Banks. Why did you say that? You're making me look like a dope!"

"Hey, wait a minute," I said in a loud voice. "I didn't tell anyone you were . . ." And then it socked me. My heart turned to stone and dropped to my toes.

Kevin! Last Saturday at Jeannie's house after tennis! I'd told him to wait and see who the committee got, and I'd said he'd be surprised. I was only trying to keep him interested in talking to me! Why did he have to broadcast it to everybody at school like it was a TV newsbreak?

Dayna was making me look awful in front of Stacey. I could feel my eyes fill with tears. *Don't cry, you nerd,* I told myself. But suddenly everything came tumbling down on top of me. I felt guilty and helpless. I had to get out of there, away from those five pairs of eyes staring at me. I pushed back my chair and ran through the kitchen and out onto the porch.

The back door slammed behind me. I leaped down the steps and raced across the yard. In the orange grove, I slumped against a tree. Twin tears, one from each eye, rolled slowly down my cheeks. I hadn't meant to make Dayna look bad. Anyway, all she ever thought about was herself, yelling at me like that in front of Stacey.

Well, at least I'm not like Dayna, even if Stacey does think I act like her. Dayna's so disorganized, it's pathetic. If I were head of the dance committee, there wouldn't *be* any rumors, just orderly news releases. But no, Dayna has to make a big mess of it!

I threw myself down in my favorite place, a big hole that had once been part of an irrigation ditch. Ever since I was a little kid, I've run and hid there when I was upset.

A cloudburst of tears ran down my face. Next time anyone claimed I was like Dayna— or Tim, for that matter—I'd do something horrible.

I heard a rustle of leaves and looked up. Stacey was standing on the other side of the ditch.

"I despise Dayna," I said fiercely. "She's such a jerk!"

"She's just angry. She'll get over it when she realizes you're not the one responsible for that story getting around school."

"But I am!" I admitted. "Kevin bugged me about the dance, so I thought he'd shut up if I hinted that the name of the band was a secret. How was I supposed to know he'd go blabbering it all over?"

"Dayna will understand," Stacey assured me, jumping into the ditch and settling down beside me.

"Fat chance," I muttered.

We sat there quietly. I don't know what Stacey was thinking, but I was just plain furious. Not at Kevin, of course. It's not his fault that my sister is paranoid about what the guys think of her.

"When we're in ninth grade, I want to be on the dance committee," I informed Stacey. "I'll get somebody sensational, like Mossy Banks.

That'll show Dayna," I sighed. "How do you get in touch with groups like that?"

I thought so hard my brain almost burst.

"Maybe . . ." I wondered out loud, ". . . maybe Jeannie's father can tell us. He owns the music store. He should know what people to write to about concerts and things like that, don't you think?"

"I suppose," Stacey murmured.

My brain cooked up the neatest daydream. I was at our graduation dance two years from now. Ian Macpherson was there with Mossy Banks, and he was telling everyone how terrific I was to have arranged for them to play for us . . . when, *wham!* A thought invaded my fantasy.

I straightened my back and turned to Stacey.

"The man at the record company. Your grandmother's friend. The one who sends you those promotional albums. He could tell us where to write, couldn't he?"

"I suppose," Stacey said very softly. But she sounded doubtful.

"You know his address, don't you?"

"Our dance isn't for two years. You don't want to write now, do you?"

"Let's."

"What are you going to say?" she asked.

"The date for our dance hasn't even been set. How can you ask a band to save a certain night when you don't know what that night is?"

I frowned and then pushed that roadblock out of the way.

"We'll ask about this year's dance! It's much too late, and they won't be able to make it, but that can be our excuse for writing."

"Groups like that don't personally answer all the letters they get. They don't have time."

"I know that. We'll write to that friend of your grandmother's. We'll ask him to forward our letter to Ian Macpherson or Mossy Banks' manager or some guy like that. It's worth a try," I insisted.

"I don't like to ask people for favors." Stacey's voice sounded strange. I looked at her and thought she was sick. Her face turned a greenish color. I started to get Mom when Stacey whispered, "I'll think it over and tell you in the morning."

Suddenly, she wasn't the same person at all. Maybe she didn't like her grandmother's friend. Or maybe she hadn't written a thank-you note for the album and felt funny about writing to ask a favor. All she had to do was say so. I'd understand.

She got to her feet and brushed the loose dirt from her jeans. "We'd better finish the

Russian Revolution."

We went back to the house. Mom was doing dishes. She started to say something, but one look at Stacey made her raise her eyebrows in a wordless question. I answered in the same way—raised eyebrows and a shrug.

In my room, I said, "Forget it, Stacey. I'll ask Jeannie's dad, or maybe I won't even do it. It's a stupid idea."

She gave me a weak smile. "Thank you," she muttered. She flipped through some homework papers. "What are you going to call your theme?"

"All That I Ever Hope to Know about the Russian Revolution."

"Oh, Laurie, you can't do that!"

Some pink began to overtake the green in her face.

"Sure, I can. Mr. Franklin will claim I'm being honest." We both laughed, and our two-years-in-the-future dance wasn't mentioned again.

After John picked up Stacey, Mom lectured me.

"You were unbelievably rude, Laurie, running out of the dining room in the middle of dinner. Poor Stacey never did get to finish her meal. I don't know what she'll think of our family's manners."

"Dayna started it," I protested.

"I'm speaking of your actions, young lady."

On and on she went, but eventually I escaped to my room. I sat by the window and stared out into the dark. Everything this last week had been twisted. On Friday night, Bob had come over instead of Kevin, but I'd had a super time anyway. And on Sunday, I hadn't wanted to meet Stacey, and yet we'd hit it off right away. And then tonight was the worst disaster I could remember. I'd been excited and happy that Stacey was coming for dinner, and then the whole evening had been a catastrophe.

Later, when I was in bed, Tim stood in the doorway of my room.

"Are you awake, Laurie?"

"Yes."

"You okay?"

"Sure."

He walked to the foot of my bed. "Don't be too down on Dayna. It was rough having the band cancel." He leaned over and rested his hands on the footboard. "Dayna's under a lot of pressure. You'll find out. Ninth grade's not that far away for you."

I turned over onto my stomach. "I have my own problems." My voice was muffled by the pillows.

"Can I help?"

"No."

How can horrible Dayna have a nice brother like Tim?

* * * * *

From the way my life was going, the next day should have been Friday the thirteenth, but it wasn't. It was just another Friday on the calendar, ending a week and bringing final exams and the dance that much closer.

School dragged.

And stony-faced Stacey avoided being alone with me until right before history. We were going into the room when she surprised me.

"I have that name for you. I found it in Granny's address book. But you have to promise me something," she whispered.

"If you feel funny about it, Stacey, forget it." I hoped she wouldn't take me seriously. "It was a stupid idea."

"What was?" Kevin's voice boomed in our ears. Stacey and I jumped guiltily as if we were plotting a revolution.

I could picture what Kevin would do if he found out what we'd planned. He'd make the *Guinness Book of World Records* for spreading gossip.

Finally, after volleyball, when we were stuffing our dirty gym suits into book bags, Stacey got her chance. She waved a slip of paper under my nose and repeated, "First, you have to promise something."

"Sure. Anything."

"I mean it. I want your solemn word that you will never, never tell where or how you got Mr. Steinberg's name and address. If you mention to anyone, even your mom and dad, that I gave them to you, I'll never speak to you again."

"What's the big deal?" I asked.

"Well," Stacey began slowly, "I had to sneak into Granny's room and go through her desk to find her address book. I felt like a thief. I don't want her to know, either. So promise, or I'll tear up this paper."

"I'll promise in blood, if you want me to." I thought for a moment. "Won't Mr. Steinberg wonder when he gets my letter?"

"Maybe. Maybe not. Just don't you tell him." Her voice didn't sound at all like Stacey. She looked dead serious.

Before going to Jeannie's, I went home and hid the piece of paper in my history book. No sane person would pick up my history book—but then, maybe Dayna wasn't sane.

A little while later I headed for Jeannie's.

My mind was spinning with an imaginary letter to Mr. Steinberg. The letter had to be dignified, mature-sounding, and intriguing. Yipes! But the biggest question of all was Stacey.

Why didn't she want me to mention her name? I couldn't figure her out. I wondered if I'd ever know the reason.

Seven

THAT night at Jeannie's—wow! Tim and Dayna (well, mostly Dayna) may be a pain, but even they could take lessons from Jeannie's twin sisters.

We were all at the dinner table—Jeannie, her mom and dad, her grandmother Collins, the twins, and me.

"Must we rush through dinner?" Mr. Collins asked.

"Yeah, Dad," Kerry began. "The movie—"

"—begins at seven." Kelly finished the sentence for her twin.

Horrified, Jeannie put her fork on her plate. "You two aren't going."

"Yes—" Kerry started.

"—we are." Kelly stuck her chin up in the air in a "so there" gesture.

I felt a little panicky myself. The twins were always doing something disgusting. All we needed was to have them in the theater.

"We're all planning to go," Mrs. Collins said calmly.

"Oh, no, Mom!" Jeannie wailed. "They'll ruin everything!"

Kerry and Kelly gave each other knowing glances and nodded smugly at each other.

Jeannie and I gobbled down our fish sticks and baked potatoes as fast as we could, much to Mr. Collins' disgust.

In her room after supper, Jeannie combed her hair and looked at herself in the mirror. "Why wasn't I born into a regular family with only one younger sister! But no! I had to be sent twins! Why did this happen to me?" She whirled dramatically so her back was to the mirror. "Why me?" she repeated.

"It isn't going to be that bad," I insisted, knowing perfectly well it would be worse. I couldn't care less what Bob thought, and maybe, just maybe, Kevin would become so fed up with the twins, he'd decide that . . . I turned off my thoughts. I felt guilty. After all, Jeannie and I had been best friends since third grade.

"And when is he going to ask me to the dance?" Jeannie moaned.

"Kevin?"

"Laurie, you're not listening to me."

I shrugged. "I don't know. He might not be going. Not all seventh graders are, you know."

"He's got to! If he doesn't ask me, I'll die!" She turned and stared into the mirror focusing on the beginning of a zit on her cheek. "This is going to be the most awful night of my life. What's Kevin going to think when he sees me arrive with my whole family? Even my grandmother's going!"

"He may not even notice," I suggested hopefully.

"Not notice the twins?"

I had to admit that was expecting a lot.

"Okay," I said, "why don't we just stay home?"

Jeannie peered at my image in the mirror.

"Stay home?" Jeannie's voice cracked. "Did I hear you right?"

To be honest, I was thinking of my unwritten letter to Mr. Steinberg. I'd never be able to pay attention to a movie and Kevin and Jeannie and Bob at the same time my mind was hatching letters to Mr. Steinberg.

Finally, we all headed for the car. Mr. and Mrs. Collins and Kelly sat in the front, while Jeannie, Kerry, Grandmother Collins, and I squeezed into the back. I felt like a squashed marshmallow, but the ride to the theater didn't take long.

Inside the theater lobby, I spotted Bob's camera case dangling from his shoulder. He and Kevin were in line at the refreshment counter. *Great,* I thought. *Who but Bub—Bob, that is—would bring a camera to a movie?* I didn't need a crystal ball to tell me this evening would bomb.

Jeannie frantically scanned the crowd in the lobby. She poked me with her elbow. "There they are," she muttered, and hurried to join Kevin and Bob.

"We're buying popcorn for the four of us," Kevin said when we walked up. I bit my tongue to stop from making a nasty dig about Bob's appetite. We'd been doing that since kindergarten and a habit is hard to break.

Kevin had on a gorgeous brown sweater that matched his eyes. My knees wobbled, and my heart pounded violently. Why couldn't I be the one who made *his* heart turn somersaults?

Kevin herded us toward an aisle just as I caught a glimpse of the twins dashing for the refreshment line.

"Laurie, Laurie!" Kerry called. We could hear her above the noise of the crowd.

Jeannie's chin rose a few inches, and her back straightened. The house lights were still on. Halfway down the aisle, Jeannie asked, "Is this okay?" Her eyes had a glazed look, and her jaw jutted out.

"This is great," Kevin said. Bob went in first, I stumbled in after him, Jeannie came next, and Kevin had the seat on the aisle.

"Keep cool," I whispered so quietly in Jeannie's ear that the guys couldn't hear.

Bob handed me a box of popcorn. "Here's yours."

"Thanks."

Jeannie and Kevin each had their own popcorn. But I noticed that Bob didn't have any for himself. His folks are divorced, and he lives with his mother. I had never really thought about it before, but suddenly I wondered if Bob had enough money to buy popcorn for himself.

I gave him a crooked smile. "Let's share. This is too much for one person," I lied, remembering all the times I'd finished one box and gone back for a second.

The twins did a little tap dance on their way down the aisle. Jeannie refused to look in their direction. They deliberately turned their heads the other way so they weren't watching us or where they were going. One of them knocked Kevin on the head.

"Oh, I'm so sorry." Kelly blinked her eyes at him. "I—"

"—tripped." Kerry supplied the last word.

"Accidents will happen." Kevin laughed, winking at the rest of us and causing my heart to melt like ice cream on a hot day.

The twins picked the row directly in front of us and climbed over the feet of some unlucky people. I heard Jeannie draw in her breath.

Before sitting down, Kelly stared at Kevin over the back of her seat. "I'm afraid the people behind us—"

"—will talk too much."

Both twins were squinting at us, their voices loud and clear.

"I agree," Kerry continued.

"They're weird-looking couples, aren't they?" asked Kelly.

I got squirmy wondering why we really hadn't stayed home. Anything would be better than *this!*

Kelly raised her eyes. "Let's get out of here fast." Probably Mr. Collins had sent an "or else!" signal. The twins did a speedy getaway from that aisle and settled for seats six rows ahead of ours.

Just then Kevin leaned over Jeannie and asked, "Laurie, what's a stupid idea?"

I looked at him blankly. "There are lots of them in the world, I guess."

"I mean the stupid idea you and Stacey were talking about."

Be grateful for small favors, Mom is always saying, and I sure was. The houselights faded just in time to save me from having to make up an answer.

"What's he talking about?" Jeannie murmured.

"Not now," I told her, hoping she'd forget.

The first thing on the screen was a notice about smoking. Then there was one about the refreshment counter, followed by coming attractions. Next was a short about *The Mystery of the Pyramids,* which normally I would have enjoyed. But my mind was jumping from Kevin to Stacey to Mr. Steinberg to Jeannie to Bob to the twins to Kevin to Stacey.

"Last chance for refreshments before the main feature," flashed before us in big purple letters as the lights came on again.

The twins popped up and raced toward the lobby. They weren't running, they were just walking stiff-legged as fast as they could. When they were even with our row, they stopped abruptly. Kerry accidentally on purpose flipped some of her popcorn onto Kevin.

Jeannie appeared to be in the middle of a nightmare. Her eyes were pinched shut, and she looked as though she hoped the floor would suddenly give way, and she could drop out of sight. I didn't blame her. I wanted to die, and the twins aren't even related to me!

Like a miracle, Mr. Collins appeared. He grabbed each girl by the shoulder and guided them up the aisle. "You've lost your chance for independence. From now on, you sit between your mother and me," we heard him say.

After that, things calmed down. Jeannie started to giggle again, probably in relief, and I decided that Tim and Dayna weren't so awful after all—well, Tim wasn't, at least. I made small talk with Bob about his photography.

"Why won't Stacey let me take her picture?" he wanted to know.

I shook my head. "She's got some funny ideas," I said, thinking about her not wanting me to put her name in my letter to Mr. Steinberg.

"The News comes out on Tuesday, and I wanted her picture in it, but it's too late now."

I looked at Kevin and Jeannie out of the corner of my eyes. I saw Kevin's hand sneak over and cover Jeannie's. It was too painful for me to watch, so I focused on the screen.

I couldn't concentrate, though, with so many ideas and questions dancing inside my head. Eventually the movie ended. Bob helped me on with my jacket. It was the first time a guy had ever done that.

Jeannie sat dreamy-eyed all the way home

in the car. She didn't even hear the jokes the twins made up about her and Kevin. Once we were in bed, Jeannie said softly, "Someday, Laurie, I hope you'll fall in love, too. It's wonderful!" she sighed.

I stopped listening. Obviously the twins' behavior hadn't canceled Kevin's interest in Jeannie. I wondered how a person could glue together her broken heart.

Eight

RAIN. I knew as soon as I woke up the next morning. I padded to the window and peered out. A soft drizzle made everything in the garden seem fuzzy. *Uh-oh,* I thought. *There goes our tennis date. Jeannie will have a fit.*

Of course the guys hadn't promised to be there, but Jeannie was hoping they'd show up anyway.

I scurried back to bed. Low giggles came from the hall, but there was no way I was going to let the twins know I heard them. I snuggled under the blankets, stared at the ceiling, and mentally wrote a zillion versions of my letter to Mr. Steinberg.

Why was I writing? I had no idea what I wanted to say. In fact, the harder I concentrated, the crazier the whole idea became.

Maybe I should have told Kevin. He's the

good one with words, but that would have made me a traitor to Stacey. My great idea had already turned Stacey into a sneak, snooping in her grandmother's desk and address book.

That did it. I'd have to write. I couldn't let Stacey become a sneak for nothing.

Jeannie finally opened her eyes. "Oh, no!" she moaned when she saw the rain. "Do you think the guys would like to come over and listen to records?"

I thought for a moment. Being with Kevin would make my day special, except that Jeannie would be there, too. And that would mean he wouldn't even realize I was alive. Why torture myself when I could be home writing to Mr. Steinberg?

"You're not going to *call* them, are you?" I let her know by my voice that I thought it was a dumb idea.

"You don't think I should?" She hated giving up on a day with Kevin. Who could blame her?

I shook my head violently.

"Well, then," Jeannie went on, "how about going to a movie?"

"We went last night." My ears listened to her words while my brain tried to cook up a good reason why I should go home.

"I know," she said, popping out of bed. "Let's go shopping! We both need a new dress for the dance."

"Why? Nobody's asked us to go."

Jeannie whirled around and collapsed in a heap back on top of her unmade bed. "Why hasn't Kevin asked me?" she demanded.

I wondered that myself, especially after last night. I mean, he'd held her hand during the movie. That must have meant something!

"Like I said, maybe he's staying home that night. How many seventh graders are really, truly planning to go?"

It took getting dressed and eating breakfast before we figured out that one. Probably about 19, we decided.

"But why can't I be one of them?" Jeannie moaned.

So, we listened to music. I felt rotten, not telling Jeannie about hearing the new Mossy Banks album at Stacey's. I just couldn't bring myself to do it. Now, with this new project of writing to Mr. Steinberg, I was stuck with even more horrible guilt feelings.

During lunch Jeannie said, "I'll bet Bob wants to ask you to go to the dance with him. But you always act so weird with him that I think he's afraid to."

"Me, go with Bub? You have to be crazy!"

"He's not so bad. He's kind of nice, really."

"Then you go with him!" I stuffed the last bite of a grilled-cheese sandwich into my mouth. I wished she'd stop pushing Bob on me. Sure, he'd be a lot better if he'd just leave that camera of his at home. Like last night. Whoever heard of taking a camera to a movie? Imagine having a camera as competition at a dance! "As long as he can snap pictures, he's not going to care who he's with!" I said. Jeannie had to agree.

I waited until after lunch to make my getaway. Mom came over in the station wagon because it was raining so hard I couldn't bike home without drowning. She seemed surprised that I didn't want to stay longer and wondered if I were coming down with a bug. When I told her I wanted to write something, she got really worried. "Homework? On a Saturday? Laurie, that's not like you."

There was no point in disillusioning Mom, was there?

In my room, with my stereo turned on high, I sat cross-legged on the floor and hoped that Ian Macpherson's voice would inspire me. On my lap I held a notebook, a blank piece of paper, and a pencil.

The moment had arrived.

Dear Mr. Steinberg:

That sounded dignified enough.

A friend of mine gave me your name.

Nope, I thought, scratching out that line. A friend? He might wonder what friend. Stacey's terms had sure made writing this letter hard.

It took me an hour and a half to finish a first draft. I wished I'd paid more attention to Miss Bobbington during English. She keeps saying that one day we'll need to know what she tries to pound into our heads. I just didn't know it was going to happen so soon.

Then came the question of what stationery to use. Notebook paper was definitely out. Mom had a box of good stuff, but if I asked for some, she'd want to know why. Tim had a stack of typing paper on his desk, but I didn't plan to type, so I ruled that out. It finally came down to Great-aunt Laura's Christmas present, pink paper scattered with pale blue flowers. The envelopes had darker blue flowers on the inside. It wasn't businesslike. Maybe it wasn't even dignified, but I had no choice. It would have to do.

I got out a ballpoint pen and very carefully wrote:

Dear Mr. Steinberg,

I am in seventh grade at Alta Vista Junior High School. Every year the ninth grade holds a graduation dance on the first Friday of June.

Does Mossy Banks have a concert on the first Friday of June two years from now? It would be terrific if our class could have Ian Macpherson and Mossy Banks play at our graduation dance.

I've read in the papers that Mossy Banks makes a lot of money at each concert. Will you tell me how much it will cost us?

I want to settle this far in advance, because I don't want our class to be in the same mess this year's ninth grade is in.

The group they had lined up to play broke up, so they've been left without a band. My older sister, Dayna, is chairperson, and she is going crazy trying to find someone to play. It's only five weeks away, so I guess she'll have to ask someone local.

I don't want the same thing to happen to our class. If you will let me know how much it will cost our class, we will start collecting money right now. The present class has $225 for dance expenses, and I know that's not enough.

Sincerely yours,

Laura Lynn Hamilton

* * * * *

The rain had pretty much stopped. I wanted
to get rid of the letter as fast as possible, so I
decided to ride my bicycle to the drugstore for
a stamp. They have one of those stamp
machines there, and I didn't want to poke
around the house looking for postage.

As I rode by the Rodney drive, I got an
awful feeling that I wasn't being fair to Stacey,
not showing her the finished letter. I hadn't
sealed the envelope, just in case I wanted to
check the spelling one more time. I braked,
swung my bike around, turned in between the
guard-lions, and, as usual, John appeared out
of nowhere. I was so used to him, he didn't
bother me. I called out, "Hi!" and continued
up the drive to the bottom of the steps.

Aunt Martha opened the door. "Stacey's
reading in her room. You know the way." She
gave me a big friendly smile.

I knocked before going in, because she had
the door shut. Stacey didn't seem overjoyed to
see me. In a way, it kind of made me mad.
After all, she didn't have to give me Mr. Steinberg's address.

"I thought you'd want to read this," I told
her, holding out the envelope. She acted as if
she didn't care.

She took it and pulled out the paper. "Great." That's all she said. I couldn't tell from the way she said it if she really meant it.

"Is it okay?"

"Sure." Then she smiled. "I don't see what harm it can do. Just don't expect anything to happen."

I carefully tucked the pink stationery into its envelope of dark blue flowers. "Was there any wrong spelling?"

"Nope." She shook her head.

"I'm on my way to buy a stamp."

"Aunt Martha will lend us one." Stacey hurried out of the room.

"Us," she had said. She didn't act upset anymore. She probably hoped as much as I did that Ian Macpherson would come. Only a wacko wouldn't want to meet him.

I lagged behind as we went down the stairs. Stacey had disappeared into the kitchen by the time I reached the bottom step.

The doorbell rang, and I headed toward it. But Aunt Martha called, "I'll get it," as she went flying past me in a big rush.

Stacey came back just as Aunt Martha pulled open the door. There stood Kevin and Bob. It sure surprised me to see them there. I heard Kevin say, "I'm Kevin O'Mallory, and this is Bob Ridgeway. We're in Stacey's class.

Is she home?"

As they stepped into the hall, Stacey nudged me. "Here," she muttered. I took the stamp, licked it, and stuck it on the envelope.

"Hi, Stacey," Kevin greeted her, his eyes on the envelope in my hand. "What's that, a fan letter?"

I gritted my teeth. Of all the people in the whole world I did *not* want to know about Mr. Steinberg, Kevin was the one. Look what he'd already done to me, blaring out about the surprise band. And what's he doing here and not at Jeannie's? Didn't holding her hand at the show mean anything to him?

"Drop it, Kevin," Bob said. He could tell I didn't want to talk about the envelope. "Stacey, I know you don't want your picture in the *News*," he continued, "but will you give me an interview? I'm going to try out for the paper next year, and thought I'd get a head start by writing a story now."

"What about?"

"How Alta Vista compares with other schools you've gone to, how our sports stack up—that sort of thing."

"I guess it's all right." Stacey looked embarrassed. Everyone stood looking at each other.

Suddenly I had no desire to go mail the

letter. With Kevin here, this was where I wanted to be, too.

"You guys go into the living room," Stacey directed. "I'll be there in a minute."

Once they had vanished from the hall, Stacey wrecked my plans. "Come back after you mail the letter," she whispered.

I didn't need any urging. I broke all speed records to the post office. I expected bells to jangle and Ian Macpherson's voice to carol through the mail slot when I dropped the envelope into the box, but all I heard was a motorcycle roaring in the distance.

The round trip took me little more than 20 minutes. I breathed a sigh of relief when I saw the guys' bikes in the driveway. They were still there. I wondered what they'd talked about while I was gone, but they told me I'd have to read it in the *News*. The interview had ended, but Kevin kept on trying to get more information out of Stacey.

"Hey," I said, "I thought this was Bob's interview."

"I was just showing him how," Kevin came back at me. "After all, I've had a lot more experience." He grinned.

"You can say that again," I mumbled. This was typical Kevin. All at once, I couldn't handle Kevin barging in on Bob's interview like that. It just wasn't fair.

"I have to get home," I muttered, confused that I would willingly walk out on Kevin. *I must be sick*, I decided.

"I have to go, too," Kevin said. He would decide to come along the first time in my life I wanted to get away from him.

Outside, I waved good-bye to John, who was clipping a few bushes. I wondered why he just didn't leave them for Mr. Green and his Evergreen Gardeners to trim. Kevin caught up with me halfway down the drive, and when we got to the road he grabbed the handlebars of my bike to stop me. My heart bounced as though it were on a trampoline.

"I want to ask you something." Kevin's brown eyes gazed into mine. I wondered if after all this time he had finally noticed me. My heart thumped so hard, I expected it to drown out Kevin's words.

"What gives with Stacey?"

Stacey! My heart kept pounding away, because in a flash I was angry. *What is it with him, anyway?* I wondered. *He'd do anything to pry. He's more curious about things that don't concern him than a cat.* I clamped my lips tightly together to show how I felt.

"You're her closest friend here," he continued, ignoring my fastened lips. "There's something weird about this setup. What do you know that I don't know?"

I yanked my bike, making the handlebars slip from his hand.

"It's none of your business," I blurted out, so annoyed with him that I forgot for a moment it was Kevin, Kevin with the twinkling brown eyes and gorgeous nose and crooked smile.

Before he could say anything, I started pedaling as fast as I could. But down deep inside of me, I wondered.

What was the mystery of Stacey?

Nine

"HEY, guys! Look at this!"

On Tuesday, Jeannie, Stacey, and I had picked up copies of the *Alta Vista Junior High News* on our way to the lunchroom. My eyes stared so hard at the front page that I ignored Jeannie.

Dayna had done it again. Her picture shared the top half of the front page with a blazing headline: DANCE CHAIR BREAKS SILENCE. The article began:

"The time has come," dance committee chairperson Dayna Hamilton announced today, "to stop those rumors that I personally have been negotiating with top-of-the-chart bands to play at our graduation dance. An unauthorized person, attending a closed committee meeting, is guilty of circulating this falsehood," Hamilton con-

tinued. "*An official statement next week will reveal the name of the band the committee has signed.*"

My face suddenly turned brilliant red. I felt sick, thinking how embarrassed Kevin must be, having broadcast the word in good faith. He must be furious. He would be finished with me for all time. Why hadn't I kept quiet and let him bug me with questions that Saturday at Jeannie's? One stupid remark got me nothing but trouble.

"Hey, Laurie, you're not looking." Jeannie stuck her copy of the *News* right under my nose. There, in the "Picture Parade" on page four, her smiling face and Kevin's perfect face shared the same photo. *A seventh grade romance?* had been printed underneath.

"Great picture," I said, my insides still in a turmoil because of Dayna. I remembered that Stacey had claimed I was like Dayna. To have her for a sister was bad enough, but to be told I acted like her—that really crushed me.

I wanted to scream. I couldn't face Kevin, I just couldn't. Maybe I could concoct a reason for eating with some of the other kids, but what good would that do? They all knew I was the "unauthorized person."

"You go on," I told Jeannie and Stacey. "I'll

be there in a minute."

"What are you going to do?" Jeannie asked.

"I . . . I don't feel good. I'm going to sit in the library for a few minutes."

"Should we take you to the nurse?" Jeannie, who's always eager to help when you don't want her to, looked worried.

"Go ahead," I urged, turning around. "Go to lunch."

A few seconds later, Stacey ran up behind me. "Laurie, don't be upset. Dayna didn't realize how it would look in print."

"I'll bet!"

"Things look different on a printed page. Honest, they do."

"Sure, sure," I said. "The famous Miss Logan, who's had a great deal of experience being quoted in the news media, will now explain that 'unauthorized person' and 'falsehood' sound different than they look in print. Ha!"

Stacey gave me that funny smile of hers, her laughing-at-a-secret-joke look. "Okay, be mad at Dayna, but you can't avoid Kevin for the rest of your life."

"Who's avoiding Kevin?" My tone of voice showed complete disinterest—or at least I hoped it did.

"Have it your way." Stacey started off

toward the lunchroom.

I took a deep breath. She was right, of course. I'd apologize, that's what I'd do. And Kevin would think how nice I was and forget the whole thing.

"Wait up!" I called, speeding after her. When we finally got to the patio, nerves I didn't know I owned rollerskated in my stomach, and I really did feel sick. I hoped I wouldn't throw up in the lunchroom. I'd die of embarrassment!

I was all set to say I was sorry I had hinted a name band was playing at the dance. I tried to slither silently onto the bench at the opposite end from where Kevin sat.

"Hi, U.P.!" Kevin called.

"U.P.?" Stacey said. "What's that supposed to mean?"

"Unauthorized person." Kevin laughed loudly. Jeannie gazed adoringly at him in a sickening way.

Bob asked, "Feeling better?"

I nodded and then quickly dumped my bologna sandwich and an apple out of my brown bag onto the table. I ate a mouthful of sandwich and pretended to silently read page two of the *News*.

"How about a hot tip on the dance?" Kevin asked. "Which band, U.P.?" Kevin, the one who caused my heart to ache—how could he do this to me? How could he torture me like this? Tears filled my eyes, blurring all the words so I couldn't read.

He'd started this whole mess. What right did he have to talk to me like that? Kevin and Dayna could be twins, the way they never thought of anybody but themselves. My insides began to boil. I stood up and stared at Kevin with angry eyes.

"It's still the same," I said fiercely. "It's still a surprise."

I climbed out of the space between the bench and the table and strode—as if I knew where I was going—away from the patio.

When I got around the corner of the building where no one could see, I leaned against the stone wall for a few minutes. Then I wandered over toward the athletic field and plopped down in a nice shady spot under an acacia tree. I promised myself I would forget that Kevin existed. I started to read the *News* to try to get him off my mind.

No such luck. In the "Seventh-Grade Quotables" column, Kevin had given a description of his dream girl:

"I'm going to be a lawyer, so she's got to be smart enough to be accepted at a good law

school. When we come home after a long
day, I want her to know what I mean when
I toss a habeas corpus *or a* cy pres *or* ipso
facto *into the conversation."*

Lawyer. I'd never thought about being a
lawyer. With my grades, I could forget it. All I
ever wanted to do was be involved with rock
bands, and I didn't need college for that. Suddenly I wondered if I wanted to study law. It
might be fun, especially if Kevin and I went to
the same school.

I leaned back against the tree trunk and
closed my eyes. Half my brain blamed Kevin
for my misery and the other half claimed that I
had done it to myself.

"Hey, Laurie, I was only teasing."

My eyelids flew up. Kevin stood there,
silhouetted against the blue sky. No Jeannie.
How had he ever managed to get away from
her? Was I dreaming? He sat cross-legged
beside me, and I knew he was for real.

"I didn't mean to upset you," he continued.
"It was all in fun."

"That's okay," I mumbled.

Just then the warning bell rang, so we
scrambled to our feet. A golden haze surrounded everything for the rest of the school day.

Some of the golden feeling tarnished at the

end of the day. Stacey, as usual, bolted from the room as though she were "it" in a game of tag. She hated the way her grandmother still insisted that John drive her home, so she always tried to get away before any of the kids came out of the buildings.

Today, though, Mrs. Blaine, the principal, had stopped her in the hall. All the teachers were concerned about Stacey, because she had entered school so late in the term. They were always asking her if she needed any extra tutoring. The whole gang had made it to the bike rack before Stacey greeted John.

Kevin watched her climb into the car. "Laurie, have you figured out Stacey?" he asked.

"There's no mystery," I answered.

"Oh, yes, there is!" he insisted. "Why did she move here when she did? Where are her parents?"

Jeannie said, "She told us all about that."

Kevin shrugged. "I'll bet there's more to it than she lets on."

That kind of upset me, knowing how Kevin acts when he gets interested in a subject.

Later, when I walked into the kitchen at home, I found Tim, Dayna, Luke, Lois, and Jason (the third Owl) holding a conference around the table in the breakfast nook.

"Hey, Shortstop!" Tim said. I shuddered and wondered what was coming. He hasn't called me that in years. "You're the first to know," he went on.

"Don't tell her!" Dayna shouted.

"Don't tell me what?" I asked.

"It's a secret." Dayna's voice sounded almost normal. "Read about it in the *News*."

"I can guess," I told her.

"Don't you dare!" Her voice shrieked again. "Just stay out of it. You've caused me enough trouble already!"

"Laurie won't tell if you ask her not to," Tim said.

"Oh, sure! Her mouth is zipped, but the zipper's broken!"

"That's rough, Dayna," Luke put in.

"I didn't mean to cause any trouble. I merely told Kevin that the band would be a surprise, and that's still true!"

"Your creepy friend Kevin didn't have to blab it all over school," Dayna snapped.

"He's not a creep."

"Stupid friend—does that suit you any better?" she came back at me.

"He's not stupid!" My vocal chords hurt from yelling. "He's brilliant, and he's going to be a lawyer!"

"Cool it, you two," Tim interrupted.

"Okay," I said. "So the Owls are playing at the dance. Big deal."

"A psychic!" Jason exclaimed.

"I thought you didn't want them to," I said to Lois. "How can you dance when Luke's playing the drums?"

Lois looked at Luke and smiled. "Why deny my class the best band in the whole wide world?"

"I can just see Dayna sacrificing herself," I told the kitchen wall. "I wish Lois were my sister."

"If you tell Kevin, I'll kill you," Dayna threatened.

"Try it!" I said. And with that, I whirled around and left the kitchen.

Up in my room, I hurled myself onto the bed and buried my head in the pillow. *I'll make a great lawyer,* I thought, *crying at every little thing.* That thought surprised me, because I didn't know I'd made up my mind to be a lawyer. *I'll surprise my friends,* I decided, *and study hard and become a lawyer. I'll even make honors. Oh, not this year,* I realized, but eighth grade loomed up ahead.

Both Stacey and Jeannie phoned me that night, Stacey just because she didn't have anyone else to call. We yakked about what we always yak about—guys, my letter to Mr.

Steinberg, finals, summer vacation, guys.

When Jeannie called, I almost told her about the Owls playing at the dance. After all, I hadn't promised not to, and she wasn't Kevin anyway. If I did tell her, though, I'd only hear moans and groans about why Kevin hadn't asked her to go to the dance with him. So when she mentioned the dance, I pretended Mom wanted to use the phone. "I have to hang up now," I said quickly.

Later on, Tim showed up in the doorway of my room.

"You don't seem too thrilled that we're playing for the dance."

I smiled weakly. "It's super."

"Are you going?"

I shook my head.

"Would you like to go?"

I shrugged my shoulders.

He wrinkled his forehead. "It's still a long way off, but if you don't get a better offer, how about being a roadie for the band that night?"

"Roadie?" I echoed him. A roadie helps a group transport the instruments, sets up, sees that the lighting is okay, runs errands—that kind of thing.

Tim raised his hand in a stop signal. "Think it over and tell me later." He turned and walked down the hall.

That stirred up my thoughts. I wanted to go all right, but as a roadie? The only way I wanted to go was with Kevin. And I stood as much of a chance of that as I did of being a lawyer.

Why not help Tim? All the guys would know no one had asked me, but so what? Life isn't a popularity contest.

Tim had gotten halfway down the stairs when I leaned over the railing. "Tim," I called.

He turned and looked at me.

"You've got yourself a roadie!" I said, laughing.

Ten

ON Wednesday, one disaster followed another. Even before I opened my eyes, a feeling of dread hit me so hard I could actually taste it. Yuck! I felt like crawling under the blankets to the foot of my bed and hibernating like a bear until after the Fourth of July!

How moronic can you get? I asked myself as I struggled out from under the covers. Of all the stupid things to do, agreeing to be a roadie was the dumbest. There I'll be, stuck at the gym from about five-thirty until midnight. There'll be no guys to dance with, no one to talk to, nothing to do but twiddle my thumbs. I moaned out loud and staggered to the bathroom.

My teeth got an extra-long brushing as I debated telling Jeannie about the Owls and the dance. I'd have to swear her to secrecy first, of course. Everyone would find out soon enough, but somehow the thought of letting her in on the deal stuck in my throat. Not because of Jeannie, but because Tim and Dragon Dayna had confided in me as if I were a real person, not just someone made up of Dayna's leftover parts.

Dayna finally called, "Mom says to come. Your breakfast is getting cold."

After eating, I met Jeannie at our usual crossroads and we continued biking together to school. Once we were in the main building, we spotted Kevin and Bob with a bunch of guys outside the door to the boys' rest room. When Kevin saw Jeannie coming, he gave a quick wave in her direction and then dashed through the doorway.

Bob greeted us cheerfully. "Hi. How are you guys?" He acted a little too jolly for Bob. Oh, he's usually friendly enough, but he's never the backslapper type, and that's the impression he was giving.

"Let's wait for Kevin," Jeannie suggested.

"Let's not," Bob said quickly. Too quickly. "It's almost time for the bell," he added. I was glad he didn't want to wait, because, truthfully, outside the door to the boys' rest room is not my favorite hanging-around place.

Stacey was at her desk when we wandered

in. "Hi!" she called out. Just after the warning bell, Kevin rushed in. He went straight to Stacey's desk without a glance at Jeannie. He looked annoyed as he leaned over and spoke to Stacey in a low voice. My heart skipped a beat. Stacey shook her head. Jeannie frowned. Now what?

By lunchtime, my insides were quivering like a bowl of half-set gelatin. Between each class, Kevin had managed to walk beside Stacey. Once, between second and third period, he grabbed my arm and started a conversation with me. He didn't say anything important. He was mainly talking about next year's senior-high football team. Then he turned to Stacey.

"Next year we'll go to all the games. Your grandmother will let you, won't she?"

When Stacey didn't answer, Kevin continued. "High school football games are the greatest. I'll just have to see that you get to them." He paused, and then acted as though he'd had a sudden thought. "Maybe if your grandmother won't let you go, you could talk your parents into it. Next time they come to visit, let me know. I'll convince them, for sure."

Stacey gave him that funny look—that private-joke look. Talking to Kevin didn't seem to bother her, not one little bit.

"When are they coming?" he pushed on.

"Who knows?" she answered.

Kevin's a funny guy. Imagine, being that determined to get Stacey to tell him about her folks. Weird, right? I wished that I could understand him.

That night I made an attempt to study, but how could I? I was all jumpy over the eternal triangle that had erupted in our class. Actually it was a rectangle, counting me.

And when Kevin phoned, I nearly dropped the receiver. He claimed he had called to check on the history assignment, but why me? Why not Bob? Or one of the other guys? For once, I had him all to myself, but then he ruined it by mentioning Stacey. It was just a rambling sentence about how nice she was and how great it was to have her in our class—and what did I know about her that I wasn't telling him?

I almost banged down the phone. If only he looked like Dracula or had a nose like King Kong, maybe I would have. Eventually we hung up, leaving me feeling weak all over.

The next day, Thursday, the *News* put out a special edition with banner headlines about the dance.

Jeannie said accusingly, "You knew all the

time that the Owls were playing. It was rotten of you not to tell me."

I dreaded what she'd say when she learned I'd agreed to be a roadie for the Owls that night. It upset me that she didn't talk about Kevin not asking her, the way she used to. She must have given up. I guess she'd cry if she talked about it.

Life was getting more and more out of sync. I had Jeannie to worry about, and I also had my own feelings about Kevin and Kevin's interest in Stacey to deal with—not to mention finals week that was coming at us fast.

That same day, Stacey and I found ourselves without Kevin as we headed for the girls' gym.

"Will we ever get an answer to my letter to Mr. Steinberg?" I asked. With everything that was going on at school, I had almost forgotten about him, especially since this year's dance seemed like a dead issue now that the Owls had been signed to play.

"The Banks are getting ready for a tour, so Mr. Steinberg is pretty busy at the moment," she volunteered. "I guess you'll hear something eventually." It crossed my mind that she knew an awful lot about Mr. Steinberg's activities.

For the next three weeks, right up until

Memorial Day weekend, Kevin acted as though a lifeline tied him to Stacey. He stuck *that* close to her side. After school, he started showing up at her house. Stacey kept inviting Jeannie and me over to study with them, but Jeannie wouldn't come after the first time.

Jeannie was shattered by Kevin's behavior. There were no more giggles. I started going home with her after school, but then she told me not to bother. She didn't want any sympathy.

For my part, it made me realize there could be a Kevin in my future after all. I felt guilty for thinking that. One part of me didn't want Jeannie to be so completely miserable, but the other part whispered, "*You* had nothing to do with the way Kevin is treating Jeannie."

My folks couldn't figure out what had happened to me. I was quiet. It was too early to spring on them that I planned to go to law school.

All the guys talked about was what to do over Memorial Day weekend. One day at lunch, Bob suggested, "How about going to the beach?"

"Okay," Kevin responded. "How will we get there?" Then his eyes looked right into mine. "I know. Let's appoint Laurie in charge of the beach party."

"Why me?" I demanded.

"Because you're good at that sort of thing—telling us what to do."

I knew what he meant—that same old bit about my interfering. And I knew what would happen. It would be the same old story. I'd make all the arrangements, and then somebody, probably Kevin, would call me bossy and say he wanted to bring colas instead of potato chips. Then somebody else would say that I had asked him to bring colas and that he had already bought them and wasn't going to switch to potato chips. Well, the whole thing would be one big headache!

On the other hand, if I didn't, no one would volunteer, and the guys would go off without the girls.

"I'll check with Tim," I said. "Maybe he can drive us."

"Will your grandmother let you go?" Kevin asked Stacey.

"I doubt it."

Nice as she is, Mrs. Logan irritated me. Couldn't she see that she was ruining Stacey's life?

* * * * *

It took a little doing, but finally Tim agreed

to drive us. At first, Jeannie said she wasn't going. She didn't want to be humiliated by Kevin. Of course, once she found out for sure Stacey wasn't going, she changed her mind in a hurry.

Stacey seemed really dejected that she wasn't allowed to go. I thought it was mean of Kevin not to offer to stay home with her, especially after all the time he'd been spending with her. I even debated spending the day with her myself. But if I did that, two of us would be unhappy. And one unhappy is better than two unhappies, isn't it?

When I woke up on the Sunday of Memorial Day weekend, mist covered the orange trees in back of our house. But by the time we left for the beach, the sun had begun to burn off the moisture.

Mrs. Collins drove Jeannie to our house. The guys biked over. Jeannie, Bob, Kevin, and I piled into the back of the station wagon. Tim brought Suzy (of the dance committee). The rest of the Owls and their girlfriends were driving with Luke.

Jeannie started off being her old self. When we were almost there, Kevin suddenly asked, "Laurie, have you figured out the mystery of Stacey yet? I know there's more behind it than she admits."

Unexpectedly, I felt a knot in my stomach. *Was Kevin right? Did I know the answer without realizing it?* I suddenly wondered. Was it possible . . . could it be . . . that Mr. Steinberg was Stacey's dad? After all, she knew all about him and what he was doing. That would explain the records. But why did she keep it a secret? It was spooky, the way she never talked about her parents.

By the time Tim parked the car, Jeannie seemed weird, and she acted kind of hyper. Even Bob became concerned. I could tell by the look on his face. I wanted to kick Kevin for having mentioned Stacey.

As it turned out, all of Alta Vista's junior and senior high students descended on the Cove that day. All the place lacked were the teachers! When we arrived, dumb Dayna was screaming louder than any of the others because some guys were chasing her. She would have screamed even louder if they hadn't.

Kevin and Bob helped Jeannie and me spread our towels on the hot sand, and then they went back to get another load of food containers. Jeannie and I took turns spreading lotion on our backs and shoulders. Someone had brought along a cassette player, so the music of Ian Macpherson and Mossy Banks and other top-of-the-charts groups blared out into the clear blue sky. It was perfect. Almost.

Kevin was up to something, and I didn't know what. He hung around me most of the time, and that made me nervous with Jeannie sitting there watching him. I got a terrible feeling of confusion when I tried to decide how I felt about him.

Bob had his ever-faithful camera along and snapped pictures right and left. He and Kevin went down to the other end of the beach to get some shots of a volleyball game. I stayed with Jeannie.

After the guys had been gone a little while, I asked Jeannie if she'd like to go into the ocean with me. "After all, that's why we came," I said.

But she refused, preferring to stare at the water from the sand and be by herself, so I went in alone. She worried me, but I didn't know what to do about it.

As I jumped over a wave, I began to wonder if maybe Kevin might ask me to the dance. Mrs. Logan sure wouldn't let Stacey go, and Kevin was pretty much ignoring Jeannie. That left me.

Without warning, Bob popped up out of the ocean beside me.

"Where's your camera?" I asked.

"On the beach. Jeannie's watching it for me." He splashed me gently, and I squealed.

Then he took a deep breath and started talking. The words came out in a rush as though he didn't dare stop once he'd begun. "Laurie, I've been wanting to ask you for a long time. Will you go to the dance with me?"

My heart dropped. Finally, someone was asking me. But it was the wrong guy. While there was a tiny squeak of a chance Kevin might ask me, I couldn't, I just couldn't, say yes.

Eleven

ON second thought, I was glad Tim had appointed me roadie. At least I had a real excuse, not a made-up one. I sighed with relief, and Bob thought it was a sigh of regret.

"I promised Tim I'd act as roadie for the Owls on the night of the dance," I explained. Then I hastily added, "He's counting on me. I'm sorry."

"I didn't know. You never mentioned it."

He seemed really disappointed, which was nice, even if it was only Bubble. I watched his shoulders sag as he walked up onto the beach. Strangely, he didn't seem like Bubble anymore. He looked like the other guys. *Why, he's as thin as Kevin! When did that happen?* I wondered. Funny, I'd never really noticed before. Something kooky churned inside of me. I didn't know what.

Then a sea monster grabbed me around the

knees and knocked me down. I came up sputtering.

"You!" I exclaimed, pretending fury, shaking my fist at Kevin, and getting dunked again. We splashed around, laughing and shrieking. I forgot Jeannie. I forgot Stacey and Bob. I even forgot the dance.

Nobody existed in the whole wide world but Kevin and me.

"Are you going to the dance, Laurie?"

I just stared at him. "The dance?" I repeated like a robot.

"You know. Music. Lights. Refreshments."

"Oh," I said, displaying true mental brilliance.

"If you're planning to stay home and watch TV, how about pulling the plug on your set and going to the dance with me?"

"With you?" I felt this tingling all over. My breathing did a skip and a hop. This is what I had dreamed of. I couldn't believe it was really happening. Kevin had asked me, *me*, Laurie Lynn Hamilton, to go with him! Kevin!

My swallowing parts didn't work right. "I . . . I'd . . ." That's as much as I could say. But something kept me from jumping with joy. How could I face Jeannie? And there was something about Kevin himself that made me uneasy. I'd dreamed of this moment, but now that it was here, it didn't feel right.

I shook my head. "I can't," I said. *Oh, Kevin,* I thought, *you should have known I wouldn't do that to Jeannie.* And now I had Bob to worry about. I didn't want to hurt him either.

I saw Kevin give a shrug and mutter, "Okay, Laurie. See you around." Then he swam away.

I staggered onto the beach and collapsed on my towel next to Jeannie.

"Bob's gone home" she told me.

"What?"

"Bob's gone home. He said there was something he had to do. I think he's sweet."

"How's he getting there?" I asked.

"On the bus."

I stretched out on my towel, feeling like a waterlogged mermaid. This beach party had become a disaster. Studying for finals would have been more fun.

After that, the afternoon dragged. I kept wondering why I hadn't told Kevin that Tim had asked me to be a roadie for the Owls. It was a perfect reason for saying no. But somehow, what Kevin thought didn't seem important to me anymore.

Kevin and Jeannie got together again when we spread out the lunches. Jeannie's deviled eggs did it. Kevin ate Bob's share, too.

After we ate, Kevin and Jeannie raced to

the rocks and back, threw sand at each other, played leap frog together—all that silly stuff. By the time we struggled into the car for the homeward trip, Kevin acted normal again, as if he hadn't mentioned the dance to me. Jeannie had the giggles now that Kevin was paying attention to her again.

As we turned onto Jeannie's street, Kevin said he'd get his bike tomorrow, because he wanted to be dropped off at Jeannie's. That made me wonder if Bob had gotten his bike at our house. For no reason at all, I hoped he hadn't.

Tim drove us up the driveway about six-thirty. Only Kevin's bike was there. I showered, washed my hair to get the sand out, then wiggled into a pair of clean jeans and a faded sweatshirt. I didn't want any supper after nibbling on junk food most of the afternoon, so I headed for Stacey's.

I walked across the grass, pushed my way through some bushes that formed a ragged hedge on our side, and climbed over the rocks that had tumbled down from the wall. My thoughts bounced back and forth between Kevin and Bob. Should I tell Stacey about Kevin asking me to the dance? Somehow, I didn't really want to.

Then I started thinking about Bob. I

wondered why Bob had taken the bus home.

I was walking along Stacey's driveway when I glanced up. My heart lurched. There, at the bottom of the front steps, stood a bike. Bob's bike. I stopped and stared at it. A whirling feeling spun inside of me.

I turned around. They—he—wouldn't want me to barge in. Suddenly I felt as friendless as a lone seagull on a deserted beach.

* * * * *

Around eight o'clock, Stacey phoned. She rattled on almost as much as Jeannie does.

"Oh, Laurie, Bob's the nicest person I know!"

"I'm glad you told me."

"You know what I mean. He came home from the beach to see me."

Well, what did you expect? my brain hissed at me. *You turned him down, didn't you?* I felt sick.

"That's nice," I mumbled.

"He thought I might be lonely, on account of everyone being with you guys at the beach. He said that when he was little and fat, he was always left out of things, so he could picture how unhappy I was. Oh, Laurie, he was so nice. He understands, even though the reason for my not going places with the crowd is different."

My stomach began to hurt again. When we were kids, even I hadn't wanted to include Bubble in some of my birthday parties. It seemed strange, looking back. I bit my lip to keep from crying.

I had missed my cue, of course. Thinking about Bob, I forgot to ask, Well, why can't you go places with us? Kevin never would have let a chance like that slip by.

I couldn't talk. "I'll see you tomorrow," I managed to get out. I felt miserable.

Memorial Day Monday was the pits. I mean the subterranean pits. I wandered around the house as though I had nothing to do. Then Dayna made one of her famous remarks. "It must be nice not to have to worry about studying. Are you trying to break the record for the most failing grades a student can get?"

That did it. Dayna made me so mad I decided I'd show her. I marched up to my room, plopped myself down at my desk, and got as far as opening my science book. But thoughts of Bob and how hurt he must have been as a kid when we didn't include him kept squirming between me and the pages.

Before, when I had been in love with Kevin, I had promised myself I'd devote this

Memorial Day Monday to cramming. After all, finals began the next day, and back then, I'd wanted to show Kevin that I, too, was smart enough to be a lawyer.

But now, what he thought of me didn't seem important. Why should I be a lawyer just because of a show-off remark of his? I made an amazing discovery. Turning down Bob's invitation to the dance bothered me more than turning down Kevin's.

I was just about ready to give up hitting the books when Stacey appeared unexpectedly.

"Out without your keeper?" I asked bitterly, still upset that Bob had left the beach to go to Stacey's.

She laughed. "Yep. John agrees that I can sneak over that tumbled-down section of the wall by myself as long as Grandmother doesn't know."

Big deal, I thought.

She wanted me to study with her and have lunch at her house. There wasn't any real way I could get out of it without making up some fantastic story. So, instead of lying on my own bed listening to Mossy Banks and dreaming of Ian Macpherson, I had to have facts that will never do me any good pushed into my unwilling brain.

Let Tim and Dayna get the super grades. I'll

let another family rake in the honors after this. I promised myself I'd never study this hard again.

* * * * *

I hadn't concentrated. I'd just sat there letting Stacey cram while I mostly daydreamed. But more must have sunk in than I'd known, because when finals began, I felt as though someone were whispering the answers into my ear.

Finals week went on forever. Actually, only three days, but three days can seem unending when they're filled with tests.

Mom had suggested that I ask Stacey to go with us to Dayna's graduation, which was sure to be boring. When Mrs. Logan let Stacey accept, I decided that miracles still happened. Stacey must have felt like an ex-con, just escaped from her prison guard.

Dayna graduated on Friday morning, and believe me, it was gross sitting there watching her get so many honors.

"Dayna bugs me," I told Stacey as we walked up the driveway to her house afterward. "It's nauseating, that's what it is. You'd think she'd be embarrassed, jumping up and down like a yo-yo because her name was called so many times."

"She must study hard to get such good grades," Stacey defended her. "She'll need those grades to get into a good college."

"Well," I announced, "I'm not going to worry about college. I'm not going. It would only be more of the same, and I'm ready to drop out right now."

Stacey grinned at me. "Oh, Laurie, you'll change your mind."

"Never!"

We went toward the house, and I noticed a big car parked by the front steps. I didn't say anything about it. It didn't seem important. But when Stacey noticed the car, I heard a sharp gasp and a low "Oh, no!" Her skin turned white and her eyes widened in an expression of—I wasn't sure what.

Then she bolted, leaving me staring at her disappearing back.

Twelve

STACEY headed toward the place where the stones had fallen down. Once she jumped the wall, she plowed through the hedge. It surprised me so much that it took me a couple of seconds to get my feet moving. With a backward glance at the car, I started off after her.

I could see her running into the orange grove behind our house. Naturally, I followed, although when she threw herself down in my favorite hideaway, the deep irrigation ditch, I slowed down. That's my "leave-me-alone" place, and something told me she wanted to be by herself. I sat down under a tree and waited.

I rummaged around my brain, trying to figure out what I should do next. I hated seeing Stacey hiding like that, yet if I tried to comfort her I would just be doing what everyone says I do too much—interfering with other people's lives.

Then I remembered that when I had been so upset over Dayna, Stacey had come after me and tried to make me feel better. I decided to follow her lead. I approached silently and dropped into the ditch across from her.

Stacey's head rested facedown on her arms, and her shoulders trembled. Every now and then I heard a little sob.

I could tell that she knew I was there. After a while, she raised her head just enough to see me.

"I hate him." She spoke in a low voice, but the way she said the words scared me. Then she started crying again. "I hate him! He's never got any time for me, but he's got plenty of time for those weirdos who hang around him. Why did he have to come?"

"Him?" I questioned. "Who's him? John?"

She shook her head. "Everyone wants to be friends with me because of him. No one cares about *me*! It's always *him*!"

What was she talking about? For the life of me, I didn't know what she meant.

She continued her raving. "Remember, I told you that I went to boarding school. I ran away. You know why? All the girls, my so-called friends, kept at me constantly. 'Stacey, get me tickets to the L.A. Forum concert?'

'How about a few freebies to the Madison Square Garden gig?' "

"Stacey," I said gently, "I don't even know who it is you hate."

"My father."

"Your fa—!" That brought me up short. I couldn't imagine hating my father.

"Everyone expects me to be like him. I'm not. What's more, I don't want to be like him!"

"I still don't understand why you don't like him. I mean, just because he works for a record company isn't a very good reason. Nobody but me knows Mr. Steinberg's your father. Nobody but me knows he even exists." Then I added, "I won't ask for tickets to concerts, honest I won't. It's not fair to expect that of you."

It gave me the creeps, the way she just sat there, not saying anything. I rattled on, "My dad's a real neat guy, but no one makes friends with me because of him."

She lifted her head, and her eyes narrowed. She peered at me as though she were trying to make up her mind about something.

"Your father's not Ian Macpherson."

The words didn't sound right. Maybe I hadn't cleaned my ears when I showered, but I thought she'd said Ian Macpherson. Then I snickered.

"Sure. And my real father is—" She looked so miserable, I stopped short.

"Why does he always have to show off? Why can't he sing without all that jumping around? I wish he were a . . . a dentist!" Tears flowed down her cheeks. "You think having Dayna for a sister is nauseating. Well, just try having Ian Macpherson for a father! It's a million times worse."

Numb from shock, I just stared at her. Gradually, the truth soaked into my brain.

"What about your dad?" I asked. "Does he know how you feel? Maybe he's hurt because you don't like having him for a father."

She ignored my question. "See," she said, "even you're looking at me differently."

"Stop being an idiot!" She made me angry, accusing me like that.

"You don't understand," she said, wiping her eyes with the back of her hands.

"Sure I do." My temper really blazed. "You're just feeling sorry for yourself."

"A lot you know about it," she snapped.

I stood up and brushed dirt from my skirt. "Look. Just remember, some of us liked you before we knew who your father is. Try explaining that away!"

Furious with Stacey, I stalked toward the house without another backward glance. I had taken about 10 steps when it hit me. Ian Macpherson is Stacey's father! Wow! He was at Stacey's, maybe this very moment, sitting in a chair I had sat in. I stumbled, the thought seemed so unbelievable. But I kept on going.

"Laurie, Laurie, wait up!" Stacey caught up with me.

Her face was still pale, but she'd stopped crying. "Listen, will you?" she asked. "When I was little, it was okay. None of the kids cared. But the last couple of years have been pretty rough. I'm never sure when kids are friendly whether or not they know who my dad is. That's why I talked Grandmother into coming here where no one knows."

"You can't run away forever," I said. "You can't pretend you aren't who you are."

"Who am I, Laurie?"

We were silent for a moment. Then I told her, "You'll have to figure that one out for yourself."

She turned abruptly without a word and headed back into the grove.

This time I didn't follow. I went into the house and slid onto the bench in the breakfast nook. *You really blew it, dummy,* I scolded myself. *You had a golden chance to meet Ian Macpherson and what do you do? Pick a fight with his daughter! Some brains you've got!*

Was Stacey telling the truth? I didn't doubt
it. No one could put on that good of an act!
Why had her dad shown up today? He surely
must know how Stacey felt. What about her
mother? Was she here, too? All Stacey ever
told me was that her mother worked. Ian
Macpherson's wife worked? How come?

I sighed, a deep sigh down to my toes. I
wanted to talk it over with someone who could
help me figure Stacey out. Bob. He cared
about people. He wouldn't go spreading the
story all over town. I half stood, starting for
the phone, when I froze. Bob, not Kevin? Why
had Bob popped into my mind first? Slowly I
sank back onto the bench.

I heard the kitchen door being opened and,
without turning my head, I watched Stacey go
to the sink and splash some cold water on her
face. I sort of expected her to be a stranger,
but she didn't look any different.

She stood beside the table. "Laurie," she
said in a low voice. "How would you like to
meet my dad?"

Grinning, I climbed out of the breakfast
nook.

"I thought you'd never ask!"

As we went down the back steps, I had
trouble believing this was really happening. I
mean, things like this just don't take place

in Alta Vista, especially to Laurie Hamilton.

"Who's John?" That had been bothering me since that first Sunday.

"My bodyguard," Stacey answered calmly, as if everybody had one.

It struck me funny, and I began to giggle. I couldn't picture me with a bodyguard.

I knew the answer, but I asked anyway. "Why did your grandmother want to know so much about Mom and Dad before you met me?"

"Oh, people are always threatening to kidnap me because Dad is famous. She worries about strangers."

We were scrambling over the wall when I said, "That's why you didn't want your picture in the *News*. Someone might recognize you."

"Right," she said.

"And I bet you'd never peeled potatoes before."

Then the wildest thing happened. Ian Macpherson must have been watching for us. He ran down the front steps, hugged Stacey and greeted me, "You're Laurie, aren't you?"

He knew me! Before I had time to say anything, he had an arm around Stacey's shoulders and his other around mine, and he was guiding us toward the house. I kept thinking, *I should have known. He looks just like*

Stacey. Why hadn't I noticed?

He was taller, of course, way taller, but his hair was the exact shade as hers. And the way he said things—his voice even *sounded* like hers! His blue eyes twinkled, just like Stacey's when she's about to laugh. Yipes! How could I not have seen the resemblance! I shook my head.

Imagine—Mrs. Logan, Aunt Martha, and John were the same as always, as if having Ian Macpherson drop in for lunch was nothing special.

Stacey asked, "Why did you come?" She didn't act as though she hated him.

"My logic may be wrong, and if it is, we can just spend the day together quietly," her dad replied. "I figured you gave Steinie's address to Laurie because you wanted me to know about the dance. And if that's true, then you were sending me a signal. Steinie recognized the town as the one you're living in, so he passed Laurie's letter on to me."

Steinie? That must be Mr. Steinberg. I was dazed for a moment, then I woke up. That's what Stacey had wanted. She had hoped Mr. Steinberg would do exactly what he did. Her dad would know there was only one way I could get that address, and that was from Stacey. *I'll bet she was testing him,* I thought, *to*

*see if he'd come. She doesn't hate him, not one
little bit. She just wants him to pay more attention to her. Poor Stacey!*

"By the way, what band is playing at the
dance?" that trillion-dollar voice asked.

"The Owls." My voice cracked, making
"The Owls" come out "The Oooowls." Was I
embarrassed!

"It's tonight, right? Are you two kids going?"

"It's Laurie's brother's group," Stacey
explained, "so she's going to roadie for them."

Stacey's father got that private-joke look on
his face. It was the same look Stacey gets.
"Think you'll need help, Laurie?"

"Oh, yes!" I answered breathlessly.

As soon as lunch was over, we phoned Bob
first.

"Come on over, can you?" Stacey asked. "I
can't tell you why, but just be sure you've got
lots of film in your camera."

Then I took over and called the Owls (not
Tim, of course). "This is your roadie. Please
be at our house a half hour earlier than
scheduled."

And when they arrived, Tim asked, "What's
going on?"

"Stacey's dad is here, and he's going to help
us tonight."

"So why the early time?" Luke asked.

"I thought you might like to meet him first. I've asked him to sing at the dance."

"You what?" Dayna screamed, having come in behind me.

"Sing at the dance," I repeated.

Tim nearly throttled me. "Great. Don't bother asking the band. Just go ahead and invite some guy to sing with us."

"I didn't think you'd mind," I told him meekly.

Dayna collapsed into the big chair. "There you go again, arranging things. Won't you ever learn?"

She changed her tune, of course, when Stacey and her dad arrived. Bob got a close-up of Dayna's face, jaw dropping and eyes popping, so I can blackmail her whenever she gives me a bad time.

Jeannie and Kevin showed up, too. After all, I couldn't leave them out. Jeannie is my best friend, but I made Kevin promise to forget the questions.

The dance that night made Alta Vista history.

When the Owls began "Touch the Night," all the kids kept right on dancing. Then Ian's voice came over the mike, followed by a moment of silence from the crowd. Then *wham-o!* The chaperons thought they might have to call the riot squad!

Midway through the dance, I asked Stacey about her mother. "You told me she works. What does she do?"

"She manages the business part of the band."

"I thought that's what Mr. Steinberg does."

Stacey laughed. "He's with the record company. There's a lot more to a band than playing music. Dad says Mom makes sure the gears mesh properly."

"I'd like to meet her."

"She's lecturing at some college this weekend. There are always some people who want to get into the business side of the music industry. She tells them what it's like."

"You mean, you can learn that at college?"

Stacey shrugged. "Some colleges, I guess."

With all the excitement whirling around me, I couldn't think straight, but I tried. Dayna and Tim never stop telling me I like to manage things. They make me feel guilty when I offer a suggestion, as though it were a bad habit.

"Music industry," Stacey had called it. What if I went to college and learned about business? If I did, maybe I could work for a band. Then my suggestions wouldn't be called interfering.

It had been dopey, pretending I wanted to

be a lawyer because of Kevin. That was like Stacey coming to Alta Vista and pretending she wasn't who she is.

But this is the true me, I thought. *Rock music is my thing. Forget law school,* I thought. *I'll major in business!*

Just then Luke gave a roll on the drums, and Dayna rushed to the mike. Yuck! Everything was super until now. Dayna embarrassed me, the way she was carrying on, flinging herself around, so I didn't hear what she said. I ran, not walked, to the nearest exit. I didn't want to stand there and have her wreck the most wonderful evening of my life.

It was a gorgeous night, with the stars shining brighter than I had ever seen them. I walked over to a low wall that separates the school lawn from some steps and stood quietly, listening to the sounds from the gym.

I can't change the way Dayna acts, I realized, *just as she can't change me.* Funny, I'd never thought of that before.

"Laurie!"

Then a different voice, "Laurie, are you out here?"

"There she is!" said the first voice.

Bob and Stacey walked over to where I stood.

Bob smiled. "Why didn't you stay? Dayna's

bragging about what a wonderful kid sister you are."

"Give me a break!" I moaned.

Suddenly Stacey threw her arms around my neck and squeezed me. "Let's always be friends."

I pulled myself away and looked into her eyes. "You're leaving Alta Vista, aren't you?"

She smiled. "I'm going home with Dad. He . . . he understands. Come visit us, Laurie."

"Sure," I said. "Whenever."

Bob tapped me on the shoulder. "Dance, Laurie?"

Then I did the craziest thing. I reached out, tucked my arms around each of them, banged our three heads together, and started to cry.

About the Author

DOROTHY HOLE grew up in Bay Ridge, a section of Brooklyn, New York. Almost every afternoon after school, she and her best friend would curl up on the floor of Dorothy's bedroom and write stories. The school she attended required a theme every Friday. "I used to wish every day were Friday," she says, "so I'd have an excuse for writing and not doing my algebra."

Mrs. Hole and her husband, Mac, now live in Altadena, California. "It's funny how my family influences my stories," Dorothy says. "My daughter and her husband are songwriters, and my husband is a photographer. Popular music and cameras are part of my daily life."

Some people think that writing is a lonely job. Not for Dorothy. "How can it be," she asks, "with all those people trying to get out of my imagination and into a story?"